BLUE DIAMOND

BLUE DIAMOND

•

Kathryn Quick

Karen —
Enjoy the
flight +
the romance —

Kathye
2001

AVALON BOOKS
NEW YORK

Published by Thomas Bouregy & Co., Inc.
160 Madison Avenue, New York, NY 10016

PRINTED IN THE UNITED STATES OF AMERICA
ON ACID-FREE PAPER
BY HADDON CRAFTSMEN, BLOOMSBURG, PENNSYLVANIA

For Mom

Chapter One

Bethany Clarke needed to make a strong opening statement—one that would leave her colleagues and the CEO of Hayes Developers with an impression of utmost competence. From her hairdo to the soles of her shoes, everything had been chosen with that purpose in mind. The overall look was professional and confident, projecting an air of self-assurance that she was the right choice for the next assistant vice president.

She opened the closet door in her office on the third floor of the Silvermeade Tower and took one last critical look in the full length mirror mounted there. The tealsuit ended just above the knees of her long legs. Her blond hair was pulled away from her face in a French twist, but the bangs that framed her eyes softened the look. She was as ready as she'd ever be. It was time to pitch her plan to save the company from the edge of the financial abyss on which it was teetering. Well, almost.

She forced herself to sort through the stack of papers on her desk until she found the second quarter report. Still gripping the cursed document in her hand, she walked over to the window, folded her arms across her chest and stared outside. Across the way she could see the sister building of the complex, the Silvermeade Shopping Plaza.

The ambitious three-part venture had been planned as a way to create jobs for its residents, tax dollars for the host municipality, and increase business for the local merchants. Phase one was the five-storied, ultramodern shopping plaza. Phase two was Silvermeade Tower, an office complex connected to the plaza by a quarter-mile long raised glass walkway overlooking phase three, a park with gardens that would put Eden to shame once finished.

On paper, it had been the perfect proposition. But then the economy bottomed out and languished longer than had been anticipated. While the mall had managed to open on time, some of the stores were still vacant. Silvermeade Tower was completed six months behind schedule, putting the rental projection figures even further off-track. And Bethany was really beginning to worry about the last remaining office suite. It was the largest, located on the tenth floor, and it had plenty of lookers, but no takers because of its expensive price tag. Not only was this the biggest project Hayes Developers had ever undertaken, but it was also supposed to be her springboard to bigger things. She was determined to save the venture and the opportunity.

As if in a trance, her blue eyes followed the movement of a yellow earthmover on the park grounds below. As it pushed around the rich, brown dirt she guessed they were working on the reflecting pool. With luck, the pool might be ready for ice-skating.

Looking farther, she saw a small figure lift up the yellow construction tape and begin to meander along the makeshift path between mounds of dirt and parked earthmovers. Beth shook her head and made a mental note to again remind her Aunt Gerry to use the enclosed walkway. With all the debris scattered around, someone could get hurt on the pathway, especially someone like her aunt who routinely ignored the obvious.

Beth walked back to her desk. Rocking back in the chair, she flipped through the neatly bound report pages, quickly absorbing what the graphs and charts told her. No matter how many times she looked at the report, it said the same thing: the actual figures were nowhere near what the estimates had been at the inception of the project. Although the economy was improving, it was improving very slowly. It would take a minor miracle to rent the last few shops in the mall and every inch of office space in the tower in time to show even a slight third-quarter profit. Since she didn't believe in miracles anymore, she closed the report and accepted the fact that long hours and long days lay ahead.

She leaned forward and hit the intercom. "Annie, my aunt is on her way over."

"Is she climbing over the construction equipment again?"

Beth sighed. "Yes. When she gets here, please send her in."

"Will do."

"Buzz me as soon as everyone begins to arrive."

Beth heard the snicker clearly. "Taken your anti-venom yet?"

"Double dosed it, Annie."

"When the company snake is in the room, you have to be prepared for him to strike."

"You know it." She laughed. The grapevine made up that nickname for Alex Kirkland for good reason. He was ruthless, determined to beat anyone and everyone to the top of the corporate ladder—and Kirkland wanted that AVP job almost as much as she did.

She tossed the report into the top drawer, knowing she had to remove any trace of anxiety from her face before her aunt arrived. Gerry had done so much for her already. If Gerry knew there were problems at work, she would want to help. But good intentions were not going to fill the offices or the stores. That hurdle was Beth's alone. Besides, there was the telegram.

She slid open the side desk drawer and retrieved the cable. Again she unfolded the yellow paper and read:

Need to see you. It's urgent. Arriving on the tenth, late afternoon. Kent McReynolds.

It was a cryptic message that both intrigued and angered her. If he had called first, she could have saved Kent the trip. There was not one good reason—short of holding the key to world peace—why she would want to see him after all these years. She slapped the note down on the desktop as memories again slipped from their place in the back of her mind and struggled forward.

The last time she saw Kent was on the day of her brother's funeral, a few days after the devastating plane crash that took his life and the life of her fiancé. Kent had assiduously avoided her until she finally cornered him in the kitchen of her sister-in-law's house. With careworn eyes that had stayed locked with hers, he held a bleak, tight-lipped expression and said nothing until she finished depositing her pain where she felt it belonged—on his shoulders.

Kent had joined the Blue Eagles, the same Air Force air demonstration team of which her brother, Steven, and her fiancé, David Mays, were already members, three weeks earlier and had been having a little trouble flying one particular formation. In a gesture of esprit de corps, David offered Kent his slot as solo plane for a while. The solo planes flew independent of the four-man diamond formation, but were still an integral part of the air show. Not three days after switching positions, the men flying four-man diamond crashed and were lost in the Arizona desert, a few miles from the air base. So in her mind, at least then, that made her double loss all Kent's fault.

She had been firm in that belief, but as the years passed, the clear-cut edges of her decision blurred and the sharp pain in her heart dulled, making the decision she reached seem nebulous.

Besides, there was more to it than that, although she hardly allowed herself to think about it . . . but today it seemed to engulf her.

Almost from the first time she saw him, Kent made her think twice about marrying David. Their sense of brotherhood, and the traditional get-togethers every Saturday night at the Flight Line Bar and Grill only made matters worse. Did her talk with David about leaving the team the night before the accident distract him and dull his reactions? Would he still be alive today if Kent McReynolds had never joined the team?

Blinking back the tears she never allowed herself to shed, she crumpled the telegram into a ball and tossed it into the wastebasket. She was not going to cry. She worked hard to bury the past and grow beyond it. She had finished college, got a degree in Land Use and Environmental Planning, passed the Professional.

Planners test and got her license, and was focused on her career, confident of her skills and intelligence.

Until the telegram arrived. Now she wasn't sure of anything, least of all what the next few hours would bring.

"Bethie?"

The voice interrupted her reflections. Beth looked up and smiled. "You startled me, Aunt Gerry."

Gerry folded herself into the chair opposite the desk, smoothing her gray skirt over her knees. Concern filled her warm brown eyes. "Are you all right, dear? You look a little pale."

Beth ran a hand across her tired brow, attempting to cover the gesture by brushing some stray hair back. "I'm fine."

Gerry reached out and automatically began to straighten the clutter on Beth's desk. "Isn't this the day Lieutenant McReynolds is coming to see you?"

"Yes." Beth's answer was more a sigh of resignation, and she stirred uneasily in her chair.

"Sometime this afternoon, right?"

"Sometime."

Gerry reached out and scraped some eraser shavings into her cupped palm. "Have you heard from him yet?" she asked, brushing them into the wastebasket at the side of the desk.

"Not yet."

"Do you think he'll be here soon?"

Beth caught herself glancing at her watch. "I don't know. The telegram didn't give an exact time."

Gerry smiled. "Maybe he can stay for dinner."

"I don't mean to sound abrupt," Beth said, apologizing ahead of time, "but I don't think Lieutenant McReynolds is going to be staying long enough to have dinner."

Gerry's smile faded a bit. "Oh." She fiddled with a

few papers on Beth's desk before putting them all in an orderly stack. "I just wondered if he might be hungry after traveling all the way from Arizona to see you, dear."

"There's an IHOP down the street. He can eat there." Beth saw her aunt look down at her hands. Over the years, Beth grew to know it was a sure sign her aunt had something profound to say. "You didn't come here to make sure I didn't push Lieutenant Mc-Reynolds from the top floor of the parking deck, did you?"

"The thought did cross my mind," Gerry admitted. "But I came to tell you I think you should hear what he has to say. It has been nearly five years since the accident, and he *is* coming all this way." She looked up, directly into Beth's eyes. "It must be very important."

Beth gave a choked, desperate laugh. "Whatever is on his mind, I don't see how it can possibly involve me."

"You know what they say: life is an adventure or nothing at all, dear." Gerry rose and walked toward the door. "You never know what's going to happen next. Just see what he has to say before you throw him out on his ear."

That ever-present credulous smile of her aunt's made Beth feel like a child again, and she had to smile back. If only she had one-tenth of her aunt's tolerance for the unknown.

"Maybe." Beth walked to Gerry and gave her shoulder a little squeeze. "And speaking of adventures, do me a favor and use the covered walkway until the park is finished. You're going to get hurt down there one of these days."

Gerry brushed aside Beth's affectionate warning with a swipe of one hand. "Nonsense. Besides, I feel as though I'm in a tube inside that glass thing between the buildings."

"You won't feel like that when the park is finished."

"When the park is finished, I won't have to use it."

Beth opened her mouth to protest but the words were cut by the intercom. "The associates are here for your meeting."

Beth walked back to the desk and pressed the response button. "Tell them I'll be there in five, Annie." Joining her aunt near the door, she gave Gerry a quick peck on the cheek. "Looks like I'm on. I'll see you at home. Love you."

"Love you too, dear. Will you be late for dinner?"

"I don't know. If this meeting doesn't turn ugly, it could just sew up that promotion for me."

Gerry stopped dead in her tracks. "I know how important that is to you. Can I help somehow?"

"No. This session is going to be a meeting of the minds." A playful smile curled up Beth's face. "I'll be bringing mine, but I'm not sure about one of my colleagues."

Gerry patted her niece's arm. "You stand your ground now, dear. You can do anything when you put your mind to it." She walked into the hall and turned back to face her niece. "I'll just put dinner in the oven upstairs in your apartment if it gets too late. I have my bowling tonight anyway. The team will go into first place if we can take two games out of three." Suddenly she narrowed her eyes, an analytical look filling her face. "Oh, but your uncle is still away. That means I have to get a sub." She looked at Beth. "You think Lieutenant McReynolds likes to bowl?"

Beth's eyebrows rose with the question. "I have no idea."

"Never mind," Gerry said, swiping at the air with her right hand before pressing the button to call the elevator. "With all the flying that he does, he probably doesn't have time to bowl much. I bet he has a terrible handicap."

As Gerry entered the elevator and the doors closed, Beth nearly laughed aloud at her aunt's spontaneous subject change. It was a trait that had taken a little getting used to when Beth moved in after the accident, but it was a quality of Gerry's that often put things back into proper perspective. Gerry was someone who never got flustered or upset, and could always handle whatever life threw her way with a smile. Beth wished she could be like that again.

As she turned to walk to the conference room, the gold nameplate on her office door caught her eye. She ran her fingertips over the raised letters. The solidness of the metal and the office beyond it gave her a purpose and a place. She was someone who designed and built things; tangible things, things with substance, things that lasted. Things that could not be taken away in the blink of an eye or in a flash of burning light.

She straightened and squared her shoulders. Like it or not, this was who she was now. Bethany Clarke, senior planner for one of the largest development companies in the country, thirty-years old, single, career-minded, driven—and possibly the next assistant vice president.

She walked down the hall and placed her hand on the door to the executive conference room. Through the huge window at the back of the building, a plane in the cloudless sky caught her eye. It cut the endless blue in half with its puffy vapor trail, momentarily also cutting away the lock she placed on the door to her memories of David and her long-buried thoughts about Kent. They flooded back into her mind like a tidal wave.

And for that split second before she opened the double oak doors that would take her inside, everything else was forgotten.

The sleek red sports car circled the parking lot for the third time. As if in afterthought, the driver suddenly jerked the wheel sharply to the right and lurched the car into an empty parking slot facing the Tower. For a long moment he just sat there, staring at the gleaming turret of steel and glass.

Bethany Clarke.

Kent McReynolds ran his hands loosely over the steering wheel before raking his fingers through his sandy brown hair. What in the world was he doing here, sitting in this parking lot thinking of making her an offer than would turn her life upside down?

He left the key in the ignition and slid easily out of the car. His gaze never leaving the building, he slammed the car door shut and leaned against it. *Ironic,* he thought, as he removed his dark aviator sunglasses and hooked them on his shirt. The one person who could help him the most probably had the least reason to do it.

He sighed deeply and let his mind drift back to when he got the assignment, only four days earlier.

Colonel Paul Brown, "Colonel Eagle" to the members of the Blue Eagle flight crew, was a politician's soldier. A born diplomat and leader, he had come up quickly from a long line of military men, and could manage to placate both sides of the table in any crisis. Never allowing emotion to stand in the way of duty, Brown was the logical choice to take charge of the Blue Eagles right after the crash. Later, he asked to stay on when his assignment was over.

"At ease, son. Sit down," he'd said, tossing the file he had been reading back onto the well-worn desk as Kent entered the office and saluted his commanding officer. "I'm sure you went over the report thoroughly."

"Yes I have, sir," Kent replied, sliding a gunmetal gray chair away from the desk and sitting down. It was a clear, concise, three-inch thick report that did not even attempt to conceal the problem. Kent read it with a sinking feeling and a sense of finality. "Finished it at about o-three-hundred."

Colonel Eagle laughed. "At your age I'd have better things to do at that hour." When Kent didn't respond, he continued. "What was your first reaction?"

Kent shrugged. "Do you think she can do it?"

Brown leaned back into his leather chair and clasped his fingers across his slightly protruding midsection. "I don't know. Maybe. Congresswoman Clancey's a tough old bird with a lot of clout. She says the Air Force has no reason to be in show business in a sluggish economy, and is determined to roll back defense spending enough to cut the Blue Eagles out of the budget completely."

Kent slouched back in his chair, his eyes on his commanding officer. "She's been saying that for what, five, ten years now? Almost since the day she got elected."

Brown took his time, got a cigarette out of the pack he had stashed in his right-hand drawer, lit it and blew smoke toward the ceiling. It was a tactic he always used. Whether it was to put a person at ease or give them time to think, Kent could never be sure.

"This time it's different. The economy's different—heck, the world is different. The D.C. grapevine has it that she might have managed to stockpile enough votes to pull it off this time."

Kent let out a low whistle. "Doesn't sound good." Sometimes before official reports were released, word got out about what cuts were made, who was going where, and who or what would be going altogether. The speculation always annoyed Kent, because although he hated to admit it, the chatter was usually right on the money.

Brown cleared his throat and leaned forward, one elbow on the desk. "Captain, these birds have been like my own since the diamond went down. That's why I need to pull out all the stops on this one." He held up his other hand in a gesture of caution. "What I'm about to propose is strictly off the record."

Kent straightened in his seat, the intensity in Colonel Brown's eyes setting off sirens in Kent's head.

"We need an ace up our sleeves," Brown continued. "I have one, but it might be too painful to play."

"Go on," Kent said hesitantly.

"A few of the other families are already on board and are writing letters of support. That will help, but you know me, I like to cover all the bases." Leaning forward on both elbows now, Colonel Brown moved closer to Kent and looked him square in the eye. "I want you to go to New Jersey, get in touch with Steven Clarke's sister, and ask her to help us save the Blue Eagles." He sat back. "Is this going to be a problem for you?"

Kent's reaction was almost instinctive. "Well, yes, it's going to be a problem for me."

He rose, walked over to the window and stared out. He didn't need this right now—or ever for that matter. He finally had his life in order. He was comfortable with his career choice, dating a girl who was uncomplicated and undemanding when it came to his flying. He was almost at peace with the circumstances surrounding the crash. Why this? Why now?

"You know I wouldn't ask you to do this if it wasn't important," Colonel Eagle reminded him unnecessarily. "I need you to do this." He slammed his fist on the desk as he sprang from his chair. "Heck, *you* need to do this." He walked over to Kent and tapped him on the chest, near his heart. "It's in here. You know it and I know it. If I asked someone else, you'd be banging down my door demanding to know why I left you out."

Kent looked down at Colonel Brown's hand. When he looked up and their eyes met, they both knew nothing more had to be said. With the deep cuts in defense spending and the even deeper ones proposed for this session, there were not many choices or chances left.

They both knew something else. Kent was a career-minded military professional, and military professionals accepted the assignments they were handed without question. He would simply have to set his personal feelings aside and get down to work.

With great effort, Kent pasted on a noncommittal smile. "When do you want me to start?"

The commander's face did not register surprise. He knew his men well. He slapped Kent on the back and returned to his desk. "I knew I could count on you." Reaching inside the top drawer, he retrieved a slip of paper. "The minute you took this assignment, you officially went off-duty. I already had the papers filled out and approved before you got here. We're on a tight schedule if we're going to have a team after this year."

"Yes, sir," Kent replied, keeping his face emotionless. Saluting, he moved to the door.

"Report directly to me on this one," Brown said. "Off the record, of course. After all, you are on leave."

Still staring at the office tower, Kent wondered which window was Beth's. In his mind's eye, he pictured a woman with pale blond hair, porcelain skin and extraordinary blue eyes sitting at a desk, unaware of what was awaiting her. A fresh pang of uneasiness shot through him with the thought. Bethany Clarke was a walking reminder of too many things in his life: painful things, exciting things, things that changed, things that stayed the same, things he had wanted and could never have.

He wasn't anxious to see her again, but the notorious Congresswoman Clancey with her sharp budget-cutting axe left him no choice. He would need to keep that in mind over the next few weeks if he was going to pull this off.

Five years. A heck of a long time. He couldn't help wondering if those years had changed Bethany Clarke as much as they had changed Kent McReynolds.

Chapter Two

Beth took a deep breath and braced herself for what might just be the most important meeting of her life. As soon as she entered the conference room, she saw that Alex Kirkland had positioned himself next to the CEO. It wasn't often that she had a meeting with Grant Hayes, but when she did, she liked to be the first to arrive and set the tone. The few minutes she had spent with her aunt had taken away that edge.

She scanned the room. Members of the planning and sales departments were milling around the coffee station. The charts she had ordered stood in the front of the conference room. The projector was set up at the far end. Everything was ready. *She* was ready.

She pulled the double doors closed behind her and crossed the room to an empty seat directly across from Kirkland. Alex jumped to his feet the moment he saw her. She knew it wasn't because he was a gentleman and a lady had entered the room, but only because he wanted to retain control of the CEO.

"Grant, you remember our senior planner, Bethany Clarke," Kirkland said, brushing dust from his navy blue Armani suit.

Beth smiled smoothly, betraying none of her annoyance. When Hayes turned and faced her, she nodded her greeting. Hayes Developers was his company. Beginning as a small business in the garage of his first home in Branchburg, New Jersey, it had evolved into a giant in the industry.

"Miss Clarke, nice to see you again."

She looked fully into his face, which was weathered by years of outdoor work. "Mr. Hayes, thank you for coming to this meeting."

"Your memo was intriguing."

Kirkland's head snapped around, the quick motion disturbing his perfectly styled chestnut colored hair. His eyes darkened to almost black. "Memo? What memo?"

"Sit down, Alex," Beth said coolly, "and have some coffee. I'm going to fill everyone in." She walked to the easel and uncovered the first chart. "With your permission," she said to Hayes. When he nodded his approval she began, and for the next fifteen minutes she held center stage.

"Which brings me to my proposal," she said, pulling out the last chart and placing it on the easel. I've only been in this area for five years, but I think I know it very well." She allowed only a trace of enthusiasm in her voice, although the adrenaline was flowing. "We need to change the spirit of the mall." As she spoke, she walked to the projector and turned it on. Flipping a switch on the wall, she raised her voice slightly to talk over the hum of the descending screen.

"People can't afford to shop at a mall that does not

encompass all areas of the economic scale," she continued, as the schematics of the completely redesigned mall appeared on the white panel. "I propose that we actively attract discount shops, craft stores, and fabric stores, and position them on the lower floor." The laser pointer sent a red beam to a large area in the center of the bottom floor. "If we put in a play area for children, here and here, I think we'll see an additional increase in sales." Beth's gaze scanned each face in the room like a minesweeper, cataloging each reaction as she described her ambitious plan. A stunned silence followed.

Alex spoke first. "Impossible." He stood and waved away Beth's suggestion with a swipe of his hand. "It'll never work."

Beth drew herself up to full height. She was prepared for this. "But it will." She let the enthusiasm filter fully into in her voice now. "This project began as an experiment, a unique construction with its staggered levels and indoor atriums. I'm simply proposing a way to make it even more novel."

Kirkland stormed over to the easel. "Here, here, and here," he said, slapping the northeast corner of the chart until it nearly toppled, "where you have the play area on the first floor and the food court on the second." He poked at the diagram with his forefinger. "That's an anchor store, that's a jewelry store and these are a few specialty shops. Where are they going? Who's going to pay for the move? Why would they want to? The mall is barely a year old, and you're proposing major renovations." He clapped his hands together in triumph. "I'd say that about wraps up this meeting."

Grant Hayes did not move. Following his lead, no one else did either. He angled his chair toward Beth and all eyes shifted back to her.

Beth turned off the projector and steadied the vibrating easel. "I don't think so, Alex." It was time to go in for the kill. She picked up the telephone. "Annie, bring it in."

Annie entered with a stack of manila envelopes in her arms. She passed one to each person in the room.

"It's all there in the envelopes my assistant is passing out," she said. "Please take the information with you, and get back to me within a week with your questions and comments." She glanced at Hayes, and relaxed when she saw he was nodding as he scanned the information in his packet. "In summary, we have plenty of vacant stores on the upper floors. I've met with the owners of targeted shops, and they are willing to move if we stabilize the rent for the next two years. The stores will relocate in shifts so that the mall can stay open. The owners of the new stores have agreed to move into their quarters quickly and keep renovations to a minimum."

Kirkland leaned over to Grant Hayes. "This will not work, trust me," he whispered, making sure Beth heard him.

"And," Beth said, staring at Alex and drawing out the word for emphasis, "the shop owners are actually excited about the plan. Many invested a lot of money when they moved into the mall. They feel this change will bring a larger customer base, and increased sales." She dug into her packet. "As for the new stores, I already have commitments from stores like Dollar Daze, The Fabric Stop, Artsy-Craftsy, The Outlet, and the Shopping Spree."

"*Discount* stores?," Alex said with a sneer curling his lip. "In a Hayes mall?"

"Alex," she said, putting on her sweetest voice, "I didn't know you were such a snob." She turned to Grant Hayes. "It's no secret how much money has been sunk into this three-phase project. The vision was to create a development showpiece, one that can sweep the County Land Development Awards next year. One section is nothing without the other. If the mall fails, it's only a matter of time before the Tower fails, too. Then there's no reason to preserve the parkland in between. This deal I'm offering will bring the shoppers into the mall, and the shoppers will bring their money."

"Are you joking? The Shopping Spree is a seconds store," Kirkland raged on. "Consumers who shop in a store like that will never venture to the upper levels."

"It's all in the presentation," Beth rebutted, feeling more confident by the minute. "If we don't treat them like bargain hunters, they won't feel like bargain hunters." She turned to face the CEO, her tone smooth and controlled. "They'll shop the entire mall. I promise you that."

Hayes was nodding his approval. "Let me run this by the Board of Directors, Miss Clarke. Well done."

But Alex Kirkland was not about to be out-done. He turned on his charm and issued a challenge. "I see you've left out the jewel in this crowning glory: the Tower and its Princess Suite. You said that if one piece fails, they all fail. Is the hotel and office center included in this master plan of yours?"

Beth stopped sorting through the diagrams and tried not to let the shock show on her face. The question could not have come at a worse time. Despite all her plans for the mall, she had not come up with a viable solution for renting the Princess Suite in the Silvermeade Tower. A sidelong glance told her Grant Hayes was listening intently for her reply. She had gained his confidence and could not afford to lose it now.

"I plan on having a signed lease for that suite within

the month," she said, hoping her face did not tell him she was lying.

"How do you propose to do that?" Alex challenged further. "No one has bit on that big price tag since it was built."

"I don't want to upset the delicate negotiations."

Hayes slapped his thigh with his right hand and stood. "Miss Clarke, if you pull this off, we'll talk in more detail about the future." He turned to Alex. "I'm sure she will have your full cooperation with this one, Kirkland."

Alex was livid, and although it showed in his eyes, his voice was deceptively calm. "Of course, Grant. You can count on me." His forced smile remained, but dropped immediately into a scowl as soon as the double doors closed behind Hayes when he left.

"Grant!" Beth spat out the word contemptuously. She walked away from Kirkland before she committed a felony. "When did you start calling the CEO by his first name?"

"Never mind that, what about all this wheeling and dealing?" His hand swept the air at the easel and then thumped the envelope on the oval conference table. "Why wasn't I in on this?"

Beth gave him her sweetest smile and said, "Because I didn't want you to worry about breaking a leg jumping off the band wagon if Hayes shot down my plan."

"How considerate of you." Sarcasm laced his voice. Alex smiled benignly. "Well, I know for a fact that no one is remotely interested in the Princess Suite. You'll never rent that floor in thirty days."

Beth glared at him. "Oh, I'll rent it. You can bet on it."

"I'll take that bet," he shot back, his voice heavy with distaste. "Thirty days. If you rent it, I'll turn in my resignation." His mouth spread into a sardonic smile. "But if it stays empty, you do. Deal?" He extended his right hand.

"Deal." Beth grabbed his outstretched hand, and shook it hard. "And I'll personally help you pack."

For several minutes after Kirkland had gone, Beth stood there, seething. There was nothing like a good office fight to get the blood flowing. But now she had another problem.

How in the world could she possibly find someone to rent the entire tenth floor within a month?

Exit number 6 on the Interstate was always a welcome sight for Beth, but even more so today. Five miles later, she eased her blue sedan onto the country road that cut the endless farmland in half and led to her aunt and uncle's place. The warm summer wind blew a small whirlwind of dust across the road, and a few cows plodded unhurriedly toward a small stream that wound like a ribbon through the pasture.

She massaged her right temple to push out the pain. Her plan had been nearly sabotaged by Alex Kirkland who, in true form, managed to complicate things by calling attention to an unforeseen loose end—the Princess Suite. She hated loose ends; they meant unfinished business and uncertainty. And she hated uncertainty even more.

Rounding a bend in the road she caught sight of the farm in the distance. The double white silos behind the old farmhouse had not been used for years, but still they stood, always the first vestige of home to come into view and the last sight that faded in the rearview mirror as she left for work each day.

She liked to imagine that they were guards, and that they had been protecting the property since King George had given it to her ancestors during America's infancy. Much like America's history, this place had given her rock-solid, deep roots—something she had needed desperately since the accident in Arizona.

She turned the car into the gravel driveway and noticed her aunt's station wagon was gone. She smiled, remembering how excited Gerry was about her bowling league. After circling to the back of the house, she grabbed her briefcase, climbed out of the car and hurried to her small apartment on the second floor. She had just put a hand to the light switch when she heard a car approach. A distinct skid as the car stopped, followed by the rev of the engine clearly told her that it wasn't her aunt coming home.

She heard a car door slam followed by the sound of distinctly male footsteps approaching the house. She slid her briefcase onto the gray chair to the left of the back door and turned with a quick twist of her shoulders. Even before she caught the movement on the large, white front porch, she knew. "Hello, Kent," she said, hoping he didn't hear the tremor in her voice.

Kent's gaze collided with hers. He shifted from foot to foot like a nervous puppy before he adjusted his expression and nodded. "Miss Clarke. Nice to see you again."

His voice was low, and Beth could hear the control the military had instilled in him through the years. "Lieutenant," Beth acknowledged, taking in the man in front of her. She had forgotten how rock-solid a military man could be. Taller than she remembered, the breadth of his shoulders under his light blue shirt seemed wider, his hips, molded in dark blue jeans, slimmer. As he shifted his weight, the heels of his dark brown boots firmly hit the painted gray floorboards of the porch. His sandy hair, regulation short, managed to look wind blown and ruffled in the breeze that came up from the field next to the house.

Other vivid impressions struck Beth when he took a step closer to her. His strong features still held the hint of sensuality that she recalled from the past. His face, still as handsome as she remembered, looked older than it should in just five years' time. His hazel eyes, guarded a moment before when they first locked with hers, now warmed as he smiled.

"I expected to see you at the office," she said, her voice almost a murmur because of the unexpected reaction she had to seeing him. She moved back to put some distance between them.

"I just missed you there." He shoved a hand into a pocket of his jeans and leaned one shoulder against a column rail as he spoke. He saw an anxiousness in her eyes, and quickly switched his approach from direct to charming. "How have you been?"

Though Beth felt totally off-balance, she squared her shoulders and faced him head on. "How did you find me?"

"I talked a woman in your office into giving me your address."

"Don't tell me—let me guess. Spiked hair, short, cute," Beth brushed her collarbone with her fingertips, "Earrings down to here. Very talkative."

"That sounds like her."

"It could only have been Annie, my secretary."

"Did I get her in trouble?"

"That remains to be seen."

Kent found himself having difficulty tearing his gaze from Beth's face. It had always been her eyes he recalled first when he thought about her. They were the most incredible shade of blue, a shade that could only be found at about twenty thousand feet, with the sun just right and not a cloud in the sky. Eyes like that could make a man forget his name and his mission.

But now he didn't have to rely on memory. With a few blond tendrils escaping from the gold hair clip, she looked exactly as she did the first day they met. He fought the urge to reach out and brush those stray locks back into place, just as he had one other time before their worlds had blown apart.

Her voice, low and tight, shook him from his reverie. "You shouldn't have come here, Lieutenant."

"It's Captain now."

Beth closed her eyes for a moment as though gathering her strength. "Congratulations on the promotion."

He nodded his thanks before letting out a long breath of air that sounded more like a sigh of resignation. "We need to talk."

"Why?"

"For starters, don't you think it's time?"

She shook her head "No. What's done is done."

"I'm sorry, but I don't agree," he countered. "I don't mean to upset you, and if there was another way, believe me I'd take it. But I have no choice. You're the only one who can help."

Beth stared into the depths of Kent's eyes and listened to him breathe for a few endless seconds while she remembered. The last time she had looked into his eyes like this seemed forever ago. *If you ever need me, just call and I'll be there,* he had whispered in a choked voice just before she slammed the door in his face. And right then and there she swore that she'd never put herself in a position to need anyone again. Much to her satisfaction, she had kept that vow.

She suddenly found it almost wickedly seductive to know that he had a need now, a need that, by his own admission, only she could fill. But despite the fact that she had steeled herself for this moment, the genuine pain she saw behind the pleading look in his eyes made her falter.

"What could possibly be so important that involves me?" she heard herself say.

"It's the Blue Eagles," Kent said, his voice taking on an ominous quality.

Beth's head snapped up in surprise when the words registered in her mind. "How could the Blue Eagles possibly involve me?"

Kent saw her face cloud with uneasiness, but he knew he could not afford to be distracted by emotions—neither hers nor his. He looked squarely into her eyes. "I need to save the Blue Eagles, and you're the only one who can help me do it."

Beth waited, not moving, not reacting, until the words stopped smashing against her. Of all the possibilities that had entered her mind since the telegram came, helping Kent save the Blue Eagles was nowhere among them. The very idea caused fresh pain laced with fear to settle inside her heart. But she couldn't let him know that. She would remain in control . . . for now.

"I don't see how *I* can do that," she said, her voice carefully colored in neutral tones. She felt herself becoming lightheaded. She folded her arms and hugged her ribs tightly, digging her nails into her sides, partly to stay focused, partly to stop herself from lashing out at him. "I think you'd better go."

"Not yet. This is much too important—for both of us. Please. I know seeing me is a shock, but hear me out before you throw me out."

Beth drew in a troubled breath, feeling her face reveal an unwanted expression of vulnerability while she deliberated Kent's plea.

For five years she thought she had put it all behind her. With help, she had learned to handle the nightmares of the crash and develop the discipline needed to block the range of emotions that thinking of Kent evoked. But her reaction to seeing him again made her realize that she had not mastered either one. She reached for her control, found it, and brought her emotions skidding to a halt.

Holding up both hands, she backed away. "I can't help you. I simply don't care about the Blue Eagles."

"You *do* care," Kent insisted. "You care plenty. I can see it on your face, in your eyes. You might hate the Eagles and not care if they've permanently grounded or not, but one way or another, you care."

"That's absurd."

"Is it?"

"Of course it is." She wished he would just get in that flashy sports car of his and leave. But if her instincts were correct, he wasn't going to go away easily. "I'm simply not interested in Air Force show biz any longer, Captain McReynolds," she said, pleased she had somehow manifested the strength of will she was trying to portray.

"So, we're back to that, are we? Can't we at least keep it 'Beth and Kent'?"

"I'm afraid not, Captain. And I'm also afraid you've come all this way for nothing."

A shallow crease appeared between Kent's brows. "You've changed in five years." There was a long pause, as he measured his words. They came quietly and resolutely. "You used to care about a lot of things."

"Captain McReynolds, we all change," Beth quickly countered. A faint tinge of irritation shaded her voice. "And as for the things I care about, well, they're just different things now." Her eyes narrowed. "But you . . ." She pointed a slender finger at him. "You haven't changed all that much, have you?" She snickered. "I'll just bet that you're not here out of compassion or loyalty—I'll bet that you're here because it's your job to be here."

"And if it is?"

"Then you've wasted my time *and* the military's."

"Are you sure?"

"You bet I am. The tricks, the show biz fluff. Who needs it? It's not going to save the world. All it does is give you a chance to walk around in a snappy blue flight suit while someone else hands out pamphlets full of rah-rah propaganda to wide-eyed people who think you're indestructible." She flinched with the rush of remembering that filled her head. "But you *are* destructible, Captain. You know it and I know it. But the big guys, the brass . . . to them, hey, lose one and you simply plug in another. It's like replacing a missing part."

Kent's hand shot out and grabbed her wrist. "When did you get to be such a—"

"Cynic?" Beth's eyes flashed. "When the Blue Eagles took David and Stephen out of my life forever." She stared into Kent's eyes, willing herself to see only the hardness of a career-minded professional, willing herself not to see the pain, the softness that was there.

Lifting her chin and tightly hanging on to her control, she met him head on. "I worked hard to put the crash and all that followed behind me. I'm not about to take the risk of ending up right back where I started."

"You might just have to take that chance," Kent said, his voice dropping and his grip on her wrist relaxing.

"Why?"

"Because whether or not you want to admit it, if the plug gets pulled on the Blue Eagles, Steven and David's deaths would be rendered meaningless."

With those words he heard a strangled gasp escape Beth's throat. It was almost agony for him to look at her, but he forced himself. He searched her face for the girl he had known briefly all those years ago, the girl he knew would help him, the girl locked somewhere inside this angry woman. He saw that girl emerge in Beth's eyes, which a moment before were the color of cold, glacial ice, now turned to the hue of a changeable tropical sky.

"Listen," Kent continued, gently releasing her, "the pilots loved what they were doing. If they were here today, they would still be doing it. You know that. We have to keep the birds flying. For them and for us."

There was a momentary silence and then a quick explosion of sobs as Kent's words, the only argument for which Beth had no answer, claimed her. She pressed her fingertips over her eyes as her mind envisioned the diamond explode into the desert sand. She wiped escaping tears from her cheeks as she lowered her hands.

She knew Kent's words were true. She couldn't let what David and Steven loved the most fade and be forgotten simply because of her anger. One part of her wanted to shout at him, to beat her fists against his chest and throw him out of her life again for making her feel so much so fast. The other part of her wanted to throw herself into his arms and let him hold her until she felt whole again. But all she could do was stare at him, uncertain of how to put it all into words.

Kent sensed a change and spoke in short, rapid-fire sentences. "I'm sorry but I had to make you understand. We're the same, you and I. We can't just walk away. We can't let this dream die."

"Kent—"

"Please. Just think about it."

"I don't know if I can."

He touched her arm to make it a more personal plea. "You have to try."

She looked down at the connection he made between them. "I don't know."

"I tried to think of other ways, but there aren't any."

"Maybe for David."

"Captain Mays was a brave man."

"And for Steven."

"Pilots still talk about your brother."

Beth acknowledged defeat with a sigh. "Maybe I can at least think about it."

"We can't let their memory die."

"Kent, I said I'd try."

"It's for all the people in . . ." He stopped, and a puzzled look crossed his face as he let his hand break the connection between them. "What did you say?"

"I'll think about it." Her voice was couched in shadows. "I want you to understand that if I do decide to help I'm not doing it for you or for me. I'm helping for David's and Steven's memory." She stood unmoving and looked at Kent with something very fragile in her eyes.

As emotions of his own overwhelmed him like a cloud engulfs a speeding jet, he simply replied, "Whatever you can give me, I'll take."

Chapter Three

Kent sat at the dining room table in Beth's apartment behind the huge farmhouse, and cut his meatloaf into neat squares. Beth sat directly across from him, elbow propped on the table, chin resting on the knuckles of her hand, watching his every move. Despite her nonchalant pose, he could sense she was tense. But on her, he decided, it looked good.

In the incandescent light, her hair looked the color of warm honey, and he resisted the urge to reach over and run his fingers through the silky strands. Tiny lightning bolts of worry darted around her eyes, making them seem even more brilliant.

This is insane, he thought. *Concentrate on business.* "Dinner is great," he said, putting down his fork. "But you should have let me take you out."

"Nonsense," she said as she rearranged the food on her plate with intense concentration. "One person could not possibly eat everything my aunt brought up

30

here. Besides, I'd rather get used to the idea of working with you in the privacy of my own home."

"So you've been thinking about the project?"

"Ever since you dropped the bombshell on me an hour ago." She put a hand to her eyes and let out a deep sigh. "I thought that part of my life was over." She spread her fingers and peeked out at him. "I said a lot of horrible things to you."

"Forget it. I have," he lied.

Beth nodded and tried to see the man rather than the memory. Intensity filtered out of his face, but in his eyes she could still see restraint. As he reached for a slice of thick homemade bread, she followed his hands, long-fingered and strong, until they returned to his plate.

"If I do agree to do this, how *do* we start?" she asked, shaking herself from her ridiculous preoccupation with his fingers, "And when?"

Kent swirled a french fry in a mound of ketchup. "I think our best approach is to deal with the person who has sights on shooting the Blue Eagles out of the sky, the one determined to bring the national budget into balance by cutting out the frills. We need to show that the team is important to America."

"How?"

Kent shrugged. "I don't exactly have a bonafide plan yet."

"I assumed this had all been worked out in some war room deep in the bowels of the Pentagon."

Kent grimaced. "Actually, I'm not sure about anything."

"Really, Captain? Where is that unshaken confidence you flyboys have running in your veins along with the ice water?"

Kent felt the smile leave his face. Her words had raked across an exposed nerve. He slid his forearms onto the table and leaned forward. "I'm not all that happy about this assignment myself."

"Then why did you take it?"

Kent picked up his fork and jabbed at his food. "Because I realized it was important. Believe me, coming here and seeing you would not be my first choice."

"It was quite a shock to see you, too."

"Considering what happened between us right before the accident, I worried about us working together."

Beth pressed her lips together and lowered her eyes. She had tried hard to forget that night, the way he made her feel, the way he touched her heart so suddenly and completely made her question her feelings for David. She shook her head to banish the thought, and discovered he was still talking.

"But then it was only one kiss." He looked at her for a reaction and saw her wince.

"Exactly," she heard herself agree. "And when this mission is over you'll fly away like a good little airman is trained to do. No harm, no foul."

"That's not fair, Beth."

"Life's not fair, Kent."

Kent held up his hands in a defensive motion. "This was a bad idea. I'm sorry."

Beth heard the tightness in his tone and touched his arm when he started to rise from his chair. For some reason she couldn't let him leave. She looked fully into his eyes and felt as if she was looking into her own soul. "Don't go," she whispered, relaxing as he slowly sat back down. "Give me a little time to get used to the idea."

"I shouldn't have asked you to do this," he said quietly.

"But you did and, like it or not, we just might have to do this together."

Looking into her melancholy eyes, he nodded slowly. "I suppose we do."

"When would we start?"

"I need to set a few wheels in motion first."

"How much help can we expect from the Air Force?"

"Not much. Technically this is all unofficial."

She laughed to cover her annoyance. "Great. You breeze back into my life, ask me to do the impossible and now you tell me it's all unofficial? What other surprises can I expect?"

"Don't know. I'm making this up as I go along."

Beth smiled skeptically and cut into her broccoli spear so hard that it ended up on the floor. As she reached down to retrieve it with her napkin, she decided that for both their sakes, one of them had to be sensible. She took it upon herself to be the one. Adjusting herself in the chair, she pasted on her brightest smile. "Truce. At least for now."

"Agreed," he replied, hoping he sounded more confident that he felt. "So," he continued, wanting to shift the conversation, "what exactly do you do in that big glass tower you work in?"

"I'm a professional planner."

Kent burst out laughing. "Bet in your wildest dreams you would never have planned something like this!"

"Hardly."

Kent latched on to the neutral topic. "What do you plan?"

"Buildings, shopping malls, parks, things concrete, solid . . ."

"And on the ground," he finished for her.

"I like watching things come to life right in front of my eyes. It's better than . . ." She stopped and avoided looking at Kent. "Why don't you go on into

the living room," she said, clearing the dishes. "I'll
bring in some coffee."

"Want some help?," Kent asked, rising.

She shook her head. "I'll just be a minute."

Kent walked through the arched doorway into the
huge room at the front of the apartment. It was homey,
decorated with big pieces of sturdy oak furniture and
homemade afghans just like old farmhouses are supposed to be. He sat down on the colonial sofa, leaned
back and hooked his hands behind his head.

"Great dinner," he called out, listening to the rustle
of silverware and the clank of cups.

Beth entered balancing two cups of coffee on a
black plastic tray, which she slid onto the oak coffee
table in front of the couch. "Thanks, I'll tell Aunt
Gerry." She watched Kent move to the edge of the
sofa and dump three spoonfuls of sugar into one of
the cups. "Aren't you afraid of getting hyper?" she
asked.

"No, It's been a long week. The combination of
sugar and caffeine will keep me awake until I find a
place somewhere in town to stay. Want some?" he
asked, pushing over the sugar bowl.

She declined. "Don't need to stay awake all night,
thanks."

"This place is great," Kent said, looking around the
room.

"My aunt and uncle made this apartment for me
after the accident." She looked at Kent over the rim
of her mug and searched his face for that familiar look
of pity everyone seemed to get whenever she men-
tioned the past. She was relieved to see that she
couldn't find it.

"It's nice." With one hand Kent raked back a short
lock of hair that had fallen down onto his forehead,
but it stubbornly fell back across his brow.

Beth sipped her coffee, watching him. Across from her was an honest-to-goodness enigma. On one hand, he was an incredibly attractive man she would become very involved with over the next few days or weeks, though one she would have never chosen to see again willingly. On the other, he was also a man who, if she was not very careful, could set her crashing headlong into emotions she was trying very carefully to avoid. How on earth could she help him and still retain her own sanity in the process? Fortunately the timer on the oven saved her from trying to find an immediate solution.

"I hope you like cinnamon rolls," she said, walking back into the kitchen. "I popped some in the oven for dessert."

"Need any help?" Kent followed her into the kitchen.

"It's your turn now," she said, sliding the pan onto a brightly painted tile hot plate. "What do you do in your spare time?"

Beth slid the plate in front of him. When she reached to close the oven door, somehow bare skin touched hot metal. "Ow!" Her fingertip flew to her mouth.

Kent moved quickly to her. "Let me see that."

She extended her hand to him. "I almost forgot— you flyboys are trained in survival techniques."

"That's right, so let a professional handle this."

The skin on her finger was red but it didn't appear as though the heat had done much damage. Unfortunately, as he held her hand, he was not having the same luck. When he touched her, it was as though the warmth of her skin had fused her hand to his own. His glance slid from her fingertips to her face, and something intense flared when their eyes met, some-thing he was totally unprepared to handle. As their gazes held, the look on Beth's face told him that she was feeling something similar.

Quickly he pulled Beth to the sink and thrust the burn under running cold water. "This should keep it from blistering."

"I'm fine," she stammered as the cool water managed to douse the fire in both her fingertip and her cheeks. She reached over, turned off the faucet and yanked herself free of Kent's hand. "I think I'll live." She dried her hand on a blue gingham kitchen towel, feeling what she could only characterize as electricity crackling on her wrist where he had held her. "Thank you." She picked up the plate from the table and walked back into the living room. "Let's eat these rolls before they cool down"

"They smell wonderful," he said, as she set the dish on the coffee table.

"Cinnamon rolls are my weakness. When I have a tough day at work, I come home, make a whole bunch and eat every one."

Kent sat back down on the couch and was struck suddenly by how comfortable he was becoming. Everything in the room seemed warm, cozy and inviting . . . even Beth. "Thanks for putting up with me. I imagine your first impulse was to toss me out on my ear."

Beth lifted her coffee cup in a toast to his honesty. "Fashionably understated."

Kent laughed in agreement. Across from him, Beth had curled up on the chair, tucking her legs beneath her and holding her cup in one hand. He guessed she had no idea how appealing she looked sitting there. Despite the fragility about her when it came to the accident and the obvious agony just seeing him has caused her, he sensed a strength about her that he really liked.

"Tell me, how much competition is there?" he asked abruptly.

"Excuse me?"

"The competition. Will I have to duel a boyfriend, fight off a serious suitor or outmaneuver a co-worker for your time?"

"Pretty direct, aren't you?"

"There's no time to mince words," Kent replied. He stretched one arm across the back of the sofa.

"You let me handle my time."

It was a warning, casual and carefully placed, but a warning nonetheless, and Kent heard it as loud and clear as if it had been the scramble siren at the base.

The rattle of a doorknob shifted both their attention as Aunt Gerry breezed into the room. "I smell cinnamon rolls. Bad day, dear?" She stopped short. "Oh my, am I disturbing something?"

"Not at all, Aunt Gerry." Beth rose and greeted her aunt with a kiss. "This is Kent McReynolds."

The light in Gerry's eyes grew brighter. "Why, yes. You're that nice young man who came to see me after Steven's funeral."

Kent extended his hand to her. "A lot of people were there."

She took his hand between hers and patted his knuckles warmly. "It's the eyes, dear. You have the kind of eyes a woman, even one my age, doesn't quickly forget."

Kent felt his cheeks warm. "Thank you, ma'am."

The man blushed, Beth realized. When was the last time she had seen a man color like that? Back in high school maybe. Seeing streak of warm pink rush across Kent's handsome face was definitely attractive. He had to go. Now.

"Kent was just about to leave."

The look on Beth's face told him not to disagree.

"That's right, I need to find a place to stay." He set the cup back on the coffee table, rose and began to walk to the door.

Gerry stopped him. "You can stay with us."

The lashes shadowing Beth's cheeks rose. "Aunt Gerry?"

Gerry's hand flew to her chest and she grinned mischievously. "Your uncle is off on one of his business trips. Mr. McReynolds can spend the night here and you can come downstairs with me." She turned to Kent. "In the morning, after breakfast, you can see about finding a room somewhere."

Beth could almost see the wheels turning behind her aunt's eyes. She started to say something, but knew it would have no effect on whatever her aunt was planning.

"If it's all right with Beth," Kent said.

Reluctantly she nodded.

"That would be fine then, ma'am. And, please, call me Kent."

Gerry walked to the door. "Come downstairs when you're ready, Bethie. I'll leave the door open."

"I'll be down as soon as I get Kent settled."

"That's fine, dear. Don't rush." Gerry looked at Kent and smiled. "Nice to see you again."

He nodded to her as she left. "Nice lady," he said turning his attention back to Beth.

"She's the best. I don't know what I would have done without her. It'll just take a second to gather up what you'll need."

As Beth walked into the bathroom to get some towels, her thoughts drifted back to Arizona. Aunt Gerry and Uncle Joe had dropped everything and rushed to help. Beth's dad needed Joe to help handle their mom and Steve's wife, so Aunt Gerry stayed with her all that day. She was Beth's shoulder to cry on and crutch to lean on. It seemed only natural to go back east afterward.

"I don't need to use your room. I can use the couch," Kent said, taking the light blue towels from Beth.

Kent's words took Beth by surprise. She hadn't really thought about it, but she wasn't sure how she would have felt if Kent had slept in her room. It was her haven, her sanctuary.

"I'll get some pillows and blankets. Let me move some of this stuff," she said, removing the colorful afghans from the sofa and tossing them to one side. "My aunt loves to make things."

"Like dates?" Kent quipped, a smile spreading over his lips.

Beth laughed. "Be careful or she'll find one for you."

"Maybe she already has." The tiny lines around the corners of Kent's eyes deepened as his smile turned suddenly enticing.

"I don't think so," Beth said defensively. "I made a promise never to get involved with a jet jock again."

"I can understand that, but you shouldn't rule it out."

"Why not?"

"Try me."

Beth narrowed her eyes in a question.

"I said try me."

Warily, she eyed him up and down. "I don't think so."

"We don't have to get involved, but let me at least be your friend. I'm not such a bad guy. I may be a bit eccentric about flying, but otherwise I think you'd find I'm pretty normal." He paused and furrowed his brow thoughtfully. "Well, maybe not. I do have a tendency to directly eat from containers, and sometimes the dishes don't get done for a week, but hey, it could be worse." Grinning he threw out his hand. "Friends?"

Her returning smile was cautious but warm.

"It could be good for you."

Beth's smile suddenly died. "No, Kent."

"Why not?"

"Because."

"My grandmother always said that 'because' is not a reason."

She whirled and turned her back to him. Taking a step away, she put some distance between them. He was too close to her. Too strong. Too capable and confident. And now he was moving too fast for her to deal with logically.

She spun back to face him. "Because I'm scared, Kent. And I'm still hurt. Can't you understand that?" She pressed a hand against her aching brow. "Don't make me sorry I agreed to help."

Beth's shaky voice made him flinch. "Maybe I should find somewhere else to stay."

"No, it's late. But we both need to step back and make some adjustments." She finished converting the couch into a makeshift bed. "Besides, if I know Aunt Gerry, she's timing me. I'd better get downstairs. I'll see you in the morning." She walked to the door and stopped. "Do you need anything else?" she asked.

"No." He moved to her and took her hand. "Are you okay?"

She saw genuine concern dart around in his eyes. "Yes." As the expression on Kent's face changed and as his mouth pulled into an expression of concern, Beth suddenly had the overwhelming the urge to lean upward and press her lips to his. Somehow she sensed he was wrestling with the same urge. "Anything else you need?" she stammered, as she saw his face slowly lower to hers.

"Just one more thing." Kent's eyes moved over her face as he spoke. The last thing he wanted to do was scare her away, but he couldn't help himself. He arched his free arm around her back and drew her to him. His lips touched her cheek first, and when she didn't pull away he traced a path to her lips. At the contact, he felt her shudder, making him wonder how long it had been since someone had kissed her. But the kiss was sweet, banishing all other thoughts from his mind.

Beth could feel strength in Kent's kiss, but also gentleness. She wrapped her arms around his neck and pulled him closer, allowing herself to enjoy the closeness.

Kent lifted his head before returning for one more gentle touch to her lips. This woman was short-circuiting his senses. This was inviting trouble, he knew that. With her in his arms, he felt as though he was soaring high above the clouds at 500 miles an hour, spinning and turning, and all without benefit of his F-16 fighter jet. When he pulled back he tried to read her thoughts through her eyes, but she lowered them and did not allow it.

"Why did you do that?"

"I had to," he whispered, pulling her back to him. "I've never forgotten that night at the Flight Line."

"This isn't wise. It will only cloud our thinking."

"Sometimes," he said feeling Beth's hands moving down his arms and knowing that she was going to push him away, "I find it's necessary to pass through some clouds to reach the clarity of the open sky." He stepped back and released her. Putting a finger to her lips, he stopped her from saying anything more. "Unless we both want it, it won't happen again."

Beth walked to the door and let herself out. On the

way downstairs, she pressed her fingertips to her lips and discovered they were still warm from Kent's kiss.

"Kent McReynolds," she whispered. "Why did you walk into my life and release everything it took me years to bury?"

But could she even try to deny that she was glad that he had?

Chapter Four

Beth sat at the table in her aunt's kitchen sipping coffee the next morning, and admitted Kent could be a big problem. The kiss they shared upstairs made her think too much about the one they shared long ago.

She gave her head a quick shake. Once again Kent had barreled into her life without warning, threatening chaos disguised as a smile. If she learned anything that day in Indian Springs, she learned that everything eventually ends. Maybe not as suddenly or as violently as her future with David had but the circle always closes and life goes on.

Kent came for one thing: to save the Blue Eagles. His candor about his mission was undisguised. There was no doubt that when the assignment was over, he'd leave.

"I think it would be nice to get to know Kent better," Gerry said, poking a spatula at the eggs she was frying. "He has such nice eyes. I remember thinking

43

when I first saw him that you could read his soul through those eyes. And he seems very honorable."

Beth laughed. "Would you rather he sneaked down here in the middle of the night?"

Gerry tossed her shoulders in a gesture of defiance. "Maybe I do." She scooped one perfectly fried egg onto a plate. "It isn't normal to coop yourself up like you do."

Kent's footsteps descending the back stairs told them that they wouldn't be alone for long. "I'm not cooping myself up," Beth whispered, "I'm building a career."

"Building a wall around yourself, you mean. That's not healthy, dear," Gerry said just as Kent walked in. She made sure Beth saw the triumph on her face at getting in the last word before setting a plate of eggs in front of Kent. "Good morning. I hope you're hungry."

"Yes ma'am, I am," Kent said, nodding at Gerry before looking at Beth. "Sleep well?"

"Fine." She hoped there were no dark circles under her eyes to tell him otherwise.

Kent turned to Gerry. "Thank you for letting me stay here."

"And he's polite, too, Bethie," Gerry said, noticing Beth's cheeks turn rosy pink. She motioned to Kent. "Dig in, and please, call me Gerry." She grabbed a mug and poured some coffee for herself before watching with satisfaction as Kent tore into breakfast. "How long will you be staying?"

"I'm not sure, ma'am."

Gerry stopped drinking her coffee. "You know, last night I thought of something I wanted to talk to you about." Her eyes narrowed, as though she was trying to put his face in another setting, "but this morning, I can't remember what it was." She flipped her hand in the air. "Never mind. It probably wasn't anything important." She walked to the stove and poured another cup of coffee. "I was just saying to my husband before he left, I said Joe, I must be getting that old-timers disease."

Kent's lips trembled with the need to smile. "I'm sure you'll remember." He finished his toast. "May I use your phone?" When Gerry nodded, he pushed away from the table. "Fine breakfast, ma'am. Thank you again."

"You should try my dinner," said Gerry, ignoring the exasperated sigh from Beth.

"The telephone's in the living room. Right through there," Beth said, motioning to the archway, trying to get Kent away from her Aunt before Gerry adopted him. After he left the room, Beth leaned toward her aunt. "Stop right now."

"I'm only trying to help."

"You can help by not helping."

"Tell me," Gerry said looking benignly over the brim of her freshly poured coffee, "what ever happened to that nice man you were seeing? The accountant with the big car?"

"We didn't share the same interests."

"What about that handsome, young doctor? The one that cleared up your ear infection?"

Beth shook her head. "It didn't work out."

"The banker?"

"Nope."

"The schoolteacher?"

Beth glared at her aunt. "He wanted to take me bungee-jumping, for heaven's sake. No more men who don't have their feet planted firmly on the ground." She paused and looked her aunt dead in the eye. "Maybe no more men at all for a while."

Gerry's innocent look was merely a smoke screen.

"But dear, this one followed you home. Maybe you should keep him."

"Aunt Gerry, you are not to do anything," Beth warned.

"I have no intention of interfering with fate. A man waiting for you is a good sign. David isn't coming back and I'm sure he wouldn't want you to spend the rest of your life alone."

Wearily, Beth sighed. "I know he isn't coming back. And I won't spend the rest of my life alone. I have time."

"But don't waste it, dear."

Before Beth could answer, Kent stepped back into the room. "Business problems. I have to go," he announced. He looked directly at Beth, drawing her gaze irresistibly to his eyes. "I'll call you later, after I iron out a few details."

"Sure, let me give you my number upstairs." As she handed Kent the slip of paper, the heavy silence between them was disturbing. *Why isn't Gerry butting in now,* Beth thought, *when she's really needed?* "Why don't we go over the details at dinner," she finally said, grasping at the only thing she could think of that sounded somewhat logical.

Gerry was nodding her heading furiously and grinning from ear to ear from behind her coffee cup. Kent almost burst out laughing, expecting her to jump across the table and accept for him. "I would like that." he said.

"Great." Beth angled her watch to her eyes and rose. "I have to be at the office in ten minutes." She snatched her purse from the counter. "How's seven o'clock?"

"Seven's fine." He barely hid his smile of anticipation as she left the room.

But Gerry hadn't missed anything. "Now that she's

gone, let's get down to some real business." She pushed back the plates and eased her elbows onto the table. "Where will you be staying, for how long, and how well do you like my niece?"

Kent's answer was instantaneous. "Probably at the Holiday Inn I saw on the way here' as long as necessary; and," the smile in his eyes contained a intense flare, "*very* much."

Kent eased his car into a space in front of the recruiting office in Somerville. The sergeant was waiting. Accepting his salute, Kent sat down in the chair opposite him.

"I'm Sergeant Lowry, sir. Colonel Brown has briefed me on the problem. I've been assigned to help."

"I guess you know this is going to be a major PR job."

"Yes, sir. The Colonel also said you were . . ." he shot Kent a knowing smile, "most persuasive."

Kent gave the sergeant a let's-get-on-with-it glare. Colonel Brown had probably gone out of his way to credit Kent's glib tongue when it came to Air Force sales pitch, probably quoting more than once the old cliché that Kent could sell ice cubes to Eskimos.

Lowry ignored Kent's glower and continued. "Congresswoman Clancey has reluctantly agreed to meet with us."

"You've already spoken to the Congresswoman?"

"That's right, but it took some convincing to get her to clear her schedule." The sergeant shrugged. "Hard to believe, but it seems that not every lady out there is in love with you guys. Anyway, she's agreed to see you Thursday."

"Terrific. And I can tell by your face that's not all."

"You flyboys are real sharp." Lowry picked up on

the scowl he was getting from Kent. "Sorry, sir." He coughed and eased back into his military manner. "At Colonel Brown's suggestion, I've arranged for you to tour a local hospital with her at a later date. We'll call the press, and she can see you in action on the ground for a change."

"I didn't want this to be a high-profile operation."

"I guess a hero's work is never done." The recruiter said, standing and offering up another precise salute.

"Forget that. I'm out of uniform."

Lowry chuckled. "Well, you'll have to crawl back into it at least for a few days."

"Not tonight." Kent looked out the large front window at the darkening sky. "If I don't accomplish what I have to do today, I'm going to be late for dinner with a gorgeous blond."

The sergeant grinned. "Take her flowers. Always works for me." He held up his hand.

Beth caught herself thinking about Kent again. She slammed the pen down on her desk, angry at her lack of concentration. Normally she never let anything disrupt her job performance, especially not a man. Not even an attractive one like Kent.

It should be easy for her to maintain control; her life was supposed to be structured around it. She had managed to avoid entanglements quite nicely so far, keeping men at an arm's length and on a social level. What made Kent McReynolds so unique?

The sound of her office door opening drew Beth away from her thoughts. She spun around to see the excited face of her secretary. "Annie, tell me that grin means it's a go!"

Annie flashed a thumbs up. "The contracts are going through legal now. As soon as some wording gets straightened out, the last store is rented."

Beth pressed her hands together and rolled her eyes to the ceiling. "Please, please let it happen."

"This should make you a shoo-in for the AVP position."

"I'm not so sure about that. It was just sheer luck that Kirkland was out at one of his extended lunches when this client came in. What I need is an ace."

Annie poured herself a cup of coffee from the pot on the credenza. "Grapevine has it there's not much competition for the AVP job."

"There's enough." Beth's brown furrowed. "Kirkland's pressing hard, and Jack Tierney sent out some feelers just the other day. I can't afford to let my guard down." With a chuckle she reached for a pen and drew aimless figures on the desk pad as she spoke. "Let's face it, Kirkland and I aren't on friendly terms since he found out I was in the running for the position."

"Watch him, Beth. He's a real viper."

Beth placed her hands behind her head and leaned back in her chair. "Kirkland can be handled, and, realistically, Tierney's too new to be a threat." She straightened, her face serious, and rubbed her hands together as her mind ran to contracts and leases. "I'd like one more big deal."

She closed her eyes as an idea began to take shape inside her head. A triumphant smile soon curled on her lips. "I've got it!" Her eyes snapped open and she snatched the newspaper from her desk. "The answer's right here."

Annie took the paper from Beth's outstretched hand and read, *"Local developer plans condominium complex?"*

"No. Right corner."

"Congressional realignment forces many offices out."

"Now follow this. Remember we were talking a few

weeks ago about how the voting districts in New Jersey were redrawn to match the new census figures?"

"Yes."

"And we thought there could be some shifting of offices?"

A smile began to form on Annie's face. "Yes."

"I was at the Planning Board meeting in Bridgewater last week to bring the township up to speed on our construction schedule, and Mayor Roberts was talking about it, too. He was hoping that Congresswoman Rose Clancey would relocate here." A broad smile spread across Beth's face. "I have the perfect place for her."

Annie suddenly understood. "The tenth floor!"

"She can move her staff *there*," they said in unison.

"There's three conference rooms, ten offices, and a corporate suite with complete living area," Beth continued. "The Congresswoman is just the kind of client we need."

Annie nodded furiously in agreement. She had been in at the start of some of Beth's ideas before, and knew that Beth's instincts were usually right on the money. It was only a matter of time before red, white and blue was decorating walls of the tenth floor. "Brilliant plan, boss," she said.

"Better than that," Beth said. She stood and walked to the window. "It's serial. The tenth floor is just the start."

"Okay, what else is going on inside that head of yours?"

"The township made us take that extra land between the complex and Route 22 when we went before the Planning and Zoning Boards. I wasn't happy about it then, but now it's perfect." She crooked a finger in Annie's direction. "Come here." Arching an arm around Annie's shoulders, she said, "Can you see it?

Right about there, a small hotel for all those important out-of-town guests and dignitaries the Congresswoman is sure to bring with her. And they'll all shop in the mall, connected to the hotel on the other side. A prosperous economic triangle surrounding some of the most beautiful parkland on the east coast."

Annie grabbed a coffee cup from the desk and raised it in a toast. "I believe we can reprint the business cards."

"Not yet." Although there was a measure of satisfaction in Beth's eyes, her voice was colored with caution. "I don't see the moving vans just yet, which is why I need you to get right on this."

Annie put down her cup. "You know you can count on me."

"First, get Mayor Roberts on the phone. Beg him if you have to, but I need to see him by tomorrow at the latest."

"Check."

"When you get him to agree, make a one o'clock at the Willows. It's his favorite restaurant."

"Check."

"Then gather everything you can get your hands on concerning Congresswoman Clancey. With the problems we've been having here, I haven't been keeping up with Washington politics. I'll need to do my homework if I'm going to rent the tenth floor and get Kirkland out of my life forever in the process."

Kent bought red roses and laid them on the passenger seat as though they were made of fine crystal. The drive to the farmhouse was giving him far too much time to think.

The Blue Eagles were the Air Force's best public relations tool. Once his picture hit the papers—and it always did when dealing with politicians—everything would be out in the open. The local paper would dig into the reason he was here and do a story on the crash, maybe even a feature on Beth's brother and fiancé.

He wanted to keep this mission low-key and stay out of uniform, to make it as easy on Beth as possible. There were just too many ways for his Eagle blues to get tangled in the way she might feel if she saw him in them. Strange, he thought as he made a right turn onto her street, this was the first time in a long time he wished he was just an ordinary guy, and not one of Uncle Sam's personality kids.

Chapter Five

Everything was ready. The roast was cooking, the wine was chilled, and Aunt Gerry was downstairs playing canasta with some of her lady friends.

Beth paced the kitchen of her apartment like a caged mountain lion. "Darn it," she whispered, walking over to the window and sweeping the curtain aside. She just couldn't concentrate on anything, and she knew all too well why. Until now she'd managed to avoid men like Kent: cocky, confident, attentive and amusing. He was no doubt overwhelming in his uniform and dangerously attractive to any woman. But he could be deadly to her heart.

She heard a car pull up outside and made a frenzied dash around the apartment before pausing in front of the mirror to smooth her hair and check for any loose mascara under her eyes. She was fine. On the outside at least.

Counting his footsteps on the staircase, she resisted

the urge to open the door before he knocked. When he did, she counted to ten slowly. "Hi, come on in."

He smiled back as he walked in, his eyes dancing with obvious anticipation. "For you," he said, sweeping the roses out from behind his back like a teenaged boy on his first date.

"I haven't gotten flowers in years."

"You haven't been seeing the right men, then," he said, enjoying the look on her face as she took the flowers from his hand. He looked around the apartment, expecting Gerry to jump out at any moment. "You alone?"

"So far. My aunt's playing cards with friends. High stakes too—a penny a point." She noticed that he had changed into a navy blazer and dark slacks. He looked very relaxed and very handsome. "Dinner will be ready in a few minutes."

A wonderful aroma wafted by his nose. "Smells great. My cooking is usually limited to something frozen you can nuke."

Beth's laughter rippled in the air. "Tonight you're getting a real dinner." She set a bottle and two glasses down on the coffee table. "Pour the wine while I finish up."

"A toast," he said, taking the corkscrew. After pouring two glasses, he handed one to her. "To your Aunt Gerry. For not allowing either of us to say no to tonight."

Beth touched her glass to his. She sipped the wine and looked at Kent over the rim. His smile went straight to her heart, warming it with the joy she saw in his brown-gold eyes.

He put his glass down on the table. "The flowers are my way of saying I'm glad we're starting over." When Beth sighed he held up both hands. "As business partners."

"Then this is as good a time as any to begin working together. You can put out the silverware."

After a moment's hesitation Kent found himself searching through Beth's kitchen drawers. In the first one he found tools, screws, glue and some wire. In another, old snapshots, but no silverware. "I would think that a professional planner would design a better strategy for her drawers," he said.

Beth glanced over her shoulder at him. "Other side."

Kent prepared himself for another hunt, but found the drawers on the right side orderly. "This is different."

"Not military neat enough for you, Captain?"

He gathered the silverware. "One side scattered, the other perfect. A little contradictory. Anything else I should know?"

Beth saw amusement come into his eyes as she set out the salad. "They say everyone has skeletons in his closet. The mess is mine." She straightened after basting the roast. "What's yours?"

Their eyes locked and held, and for a split second, Kent suddenly looked incredibly tired. There was a darkness in his eyes and a fleeting flash of pain on his face. Quickly he lowered his head and studied his shoes. "Oh, I have one or two," he replied. "But if I tell you, there won't be anything for you to find out about me, will there?"

Beth brushed away the hair that fell into her eyes. "Typical jet jock." She shook her head and snickered. "You guys never confide in anyone, much less a woman."

"I'm not that typical."

"Hmm." She studied him. There was a touch of anxiety in his eyes, but otherwise she could sense no difference between him and every other pilot she once knew. "See if this fits the profile. Flying is your one and only love and you don't worry about anything once you're airborne." She found the lump forming in her throat a little hard to swallow, but she managed to say tautly, "Not even the fact that you might not be coming back. There's no room in your life for anything but the sky, otherwise you wouldn't be here trying to make sure that the Blue Eagles can still fly after this year. Am I close?"

"No, and if you'd give me a chance, you'd see that."

Beth tipped her head back and placed a hand on one hip. "Some classic psychology tactics? I learned mine in college, where did you learn yours? Anti-terrorist training?"

Kent's eyes darkened. "Okay, it looks like it's time we got down to the rules of this encounter."

"What kind of rules?"

Ignoring the question, he took her hand and gently pulled her into the living room. "At Ops nobody tells anyone how they feel or why they feel." He took her by the arms, swung her around and deposited her on the sofa. Taking a seat on the footstool directly opposite her, he felt his expression begin to close and shook his head to stop it. "You can't take the chance of appearing insecure. The competition is so great that any edge a pilot gets could make a difference in his career; even if it is at the cost of someone else's."

"Even with feelings?"

"Especially with feelings."

She realized that she'd hit a nerve, a very raw nerve. She pressed her hands together. "I know that being a pilot is an exacting job with no room for anything but military cool."

"Right." It sounded a little sarcastic. Kent licked his bottom lip, the words coming slowly, haltingly. "Maybe most guys could, but I could never separate how I felt from what I was." He looked at the ceiling and blew out a long breath of air.

Beth grew very quiet as she watched Kent struggle. She wouldn't have thought this of him, or of anyone in a fighter unit. They knew the dangers and accepted them with the wings they had pinned to their chests. "What happened?"

"Fighter pilots are supposed to understand that death is just the cost of doing business." He tapped his temple with his forefinger. "Up here I'm supposed to understand that, but I don't. It doesn't register that way for me. If that makes me weak, then so be it." He shut his eyes, holding back the sting of tears that always made him feel inadequate when he thought back to that day. Opening his eyes, he looked at Beth but saw only the past. "I was safe at the base when it happened. I should have been there with the diamond."

Beth put her hand on his arm, feeling his muscles tense at her touch. "Kent, you don't have to tell me this."

He closed his hand over hers. "Yes, I do."

"There was nothing you could have done. I realize that now. I should never have blamed you." Her fingers tightened as she saw his eyes yield. His vulnerability and his trust in her to reveal it instantly touched her.

"I'll never know for sure if I could have made a difference." Kent blinked his eyes several times, his throat constricting, his words strained. "Possibly a low fly-by could have saved one . . . two, maybe."

Beth pressed her free hand to her mouth. She had never seen her brother or David lower their guard and allow their feelings to pour out like this. She touched his cheek. "It was a mad race to the ground," she whispered, "you would have only succeeded in killing yourself trying to save them."

Forcing his emotions back into place, Kent became all too aware of Beth's warm, assuring touch. He looked into her eyes and found tears. He wanted to kiss them away as they ran down her cheeks, but instead wiped them away with his fingertips.

"The Air Force gave me a desk to fly after the accident," he continued. "A staff job at Langley in Virginia."

"But you're still flying."

"The assignment was a disaster. I drove everyone around me crazy." He cocked a thumb upward, his tight expression relaxing. "I had to either go back up or get out."

Beth raised her eyebrows, a soft smile touching her lips. She leaned forward and looked intently over his shoulder.

Kent frowned in surprise, his eyes level under drawn brows. "What are you doing?" he asked.

"Checking."

"For what?" He twisted to the right to see what she was looking at.

"Your wings. They're there, flight feathers full and ready for take-off." She squeezed his hand to give him strength, and turned her smile up a notch. "And you try to tell me that you're not typical."

Kent stared at her and then burst out laughing. "You're amazing." He suddenly felt safe, able to show the emotions he kept bottled up and so carefully hidden from everyone else.

"I am sorry," she said. "I didn't mean to dredge up old memories."

"It's okay. Now we're even. But let's stop here."

"All this soul-searching making you feel a little stressed?"

Kent reached out and traced the path her tears had taken only a moment before. "No, it feels good."

Need simmered in Kent's voice, cutting through all Beth's defenses. She could feel the telltale heat in her face. She couldn't give away this part of herself again.

"Do you know how beautiful you are?" Kent chose his words carefully. "Your hair, your incredible eyes the color of blue diamonds. You remind me of a priceless china doll."

Shaken by his words, Beth looked away. David used to tell her that. Since Kent reappeared, the memory of the little things David used to say and do were coming back to haunt her.

"You're wrong," she said with a nervous laugh. "I didn't get to where I am today by being made of glass." She lowered her eyes and toyed with the napkin.

Kent came around the coffee table and sat down beside her. Placing a finger beneath her chin he raised her face and searched her somber-looking features. "I know that. How you ever had the guts to agree to help me, I'll never know." He thought of the sky, of the risks he took each time he climbed into the cockpit of his fighter plane. It was nothing compared to the risk he was about to take now. "We could be good for each other."

Silently Beth considered his words. He was a very dangerous man. "I don't think I can give you anything but friendship."

"Let me try to change your mind," Kent pleaded. He didn't want just now, he wanted tomorrow and the tomorrow after that.

"I can't let this happen." Putting a hand to his chest, she held him at a safe distance.

"Can't," he challenged, "or won't?"

"Both." She averted her eyes and looked past him, seeing curls of smoke coming from the oven. "I'm afraid dinner is ruined. And it's too late to start something else." Slowly, very slowly, regaining her composure, she refused him. Kent realized Beth was back on automatic. He would have to be patient. "Let me make this up to the you sometime."

"I don't think I'd be very good on a date."

"I'll take my chances."

"I'm sorry I ruined your evening," Beth said quietly.

Kent traced the curve of her cheeks with his fingertip. "You didn't."

"I'd still like to help you, but only as your friend."

At the door Kent extended his hand. "Sure. Friends then." As their hands touched, Kent pulled her to him and kissed her lightly on the cheek. "But remember, friends are allowed spontaneous bursts of affection." Then without giving her time to the protest, he was gone.

When the door closed Beth leaned back against the frame and, folding her arms across her chest, stared off into space. She had told herself from the beginning that he would mean nothing to her, but her emotions were screaming otherwise. *Funny,* she thought, picking up Kent's wineglass and running her finger around the rim. *Tonight, dinner was not the only thing that had been ruined.* Her preconceived image that all career pilots were impersonal and unaffected had just dissolved right before her eyes.

Chapter Six

Two days later, Beth still hadn't heard from Kent. Disappointed, she decided to throw herself into her dealings with Congresswoman Clancey. She had almost succeeded in taking her mind off him when the drone of the intercom broke her concentration.

"A Mr. Kent McReynolds is here to see you," Annie's clear, crisp voice said through the system.

Beth stared at the telephone, wondering if she should send him away. "Send him in, Annie," she heard herself say.

Kent pushed open the door and walked in. He spun in a small circle as he looked around the spacious office. "I'm impressed."

He toured the richly decorated suite, running his hand over some of the furnishings. "This is quite a place."

"Thanks. Please, sit down." She gathered some papers to center herself. "I thought I'd hear from you before today."

He slipped easily into the leather chair across from her and slid back in the chair, crossing his legs. "I've been busy trying to set up an appointment with our hatchetman, and I needed to stay focused."

"So you do have a plan after all."

Kent nodded. "We need some heavy-duty PR, and then a meeting where you and I can work together to make sure the Blue Eagles' wings aren't clipped too far back." He raised his eyebrows questioningly. "That is, if you haven't changed your mind."

"No, I haven't."

"Good. I need you. And I apologize—I shouldn't have burdened you with my ghosts. I came here with a mission, got sidetracked and took you with me. For that I am sorry."

"So, you're apologizing?"

"So, you're accepting?"

"No."

Kent pushed back in the seat in shock and held up his hands defensively. "The least you could do is let me finish before you toss my out on my rudder."

"It's a vertical stabilizer," she said seriously.

Kent stared at her. "What?"

"You toss a pilot out on his vertical stabilizer, not on his rudder. You should know that, Captain." She was teasing him, affectionately, not maliciously, and they both knew it. "There's no need for an apology," she said. "It was a very emotional situation at Indian Springs." She smiled and leaned back into her chair. "Besides, if you remember, I really didn't try very hard to stop you."

Kent grinned broadly. "Been quite a time, hasn't it?"

"Has it ever," she agreed. "But I think we have the

ground rules down now, so let's just call that evening an aborted try. I still owe you a meal, and I'd suggest lunch today, but just look at this mess." She swept her hand in the air above her desktop. "Every paper, a problem. Besides, I have to keep the time free for a possible last-minute lunch meeting."

"Good, because I have business lunch today myself. How about dinner tomorrow?" he quickly suggested.

"Tomorrow's fine."

"But this time, neutral ground," he suggested. "We eat out, but the restaurant is up to you."

Just then the intercom rang again. "Beth, Mayor Roberts on line one, and Kirkland's holding on two."

Beth acknowledged Annie's message as Kent appraised her tight features. "Sounds like a bad day in the making."

She ran her fingers through her blond hair and rubbed her scalp to try and ease the pain of the headache that was beginning. "Lately there seems to be no end to the problems."

"I can get rid of one of them for you right now." He cocked a thumb in his direction. "I'm your only *real* problem, anyway. I like you and, whether you're ready to admit it or not, you like me. Now that's one big dilemma to tackle."

She laughed in response; her mood seemed suddenly buoyant. "As I said, no lack of problems these days."

She walked with him to the office door where he turned and placed his hands on her arms. "You've come a long way. I know you can do anything you set your mind to." Reluctantly he stepped back and looked deeply into her crystal clear, blue eyes.

"Thanks for the support. It feels good," she admitted.

Controlling the urge to take her back in his arms, he just stood there. "If I can help, just ask."

"Sure."

"I mean it, I'm yours for the taking."

"Coming from any other man, that would be a line, Captain."

Kent laughed at her and stepped into the hall. "I guess it would." He studied her thoughtfully for a moment and then winked. "Now get to work and prove I'm right about you."

As he walked toward the elevator, Beth couldn't resist another glance in his direction. When she turned back slowly, the delight on her face was obvious to Annie, who had been walking down the hallway.

Annie's curiosity exploded. "Is he business or pleasure?"

Beth could not decide. Her answer to Annie came in a simple wink as she walked into her office and closed the door.

"Pelligrino with a twist of lime," Beth said as the Mayor ordered an iced tea.

"So tell me, Miss Clarke," Mayor Roberts said after acknowledging an associate to his right with a wave, "what's so urgent that I had to drop everything and meet you for lunch? Miss Potts sounded as though it was a matter of life and death." He looked up from the menu and studied her over the rim of his glasses. "I can't imagine what else your development firm could possibly have in store for the residents of my town."

Beth set down her mineral water. "I put my secretary up to that little charade."

The mayor sipped his drink. "Really? Let me tell you right up front, I'm not about to cut Hayes Developers any tax breaks."

"And I'm not about to ask for any."

"Good, at least we agree on that. So, why are we here?"

The mayor eyed Beth curiously. She ran a finger around the rim of her water glass, while tying up the last minute details of how she was going to bring up the matter of Congresswoman Clancey. The direct approach, the technique Kent always seemed to use, was the only way to go, she decided. "I'd like to meet a friend of yours. Congresswoman Clancey."

Mayor Roberts' eyebrows rose in surprise. "Going for the big guns, huh? I must warn you, Rosie is a tough one. And she usually doesn't bestow favors."

"It's not a favor I want. It's an opportunity. Maybe for us both. And it all starts with an introduction from you for a chance to get her to consider the Silvermeade complex as a possible site for her district office."

"Interesting. Do you think Silvermeade would suit her?"

Beth rested her forearms on the table and leaned forward. "Why not? It's in the heart of the new congressional district, it's close to major highways, easily accessible to airports, driving distance from New York and Philadelphia . . ."

"Whoa, hold on." Mayor Roberts held up his hand. "I'm not the one who needs convincing."

"Then you'll consider my request?"

The mayor looked around the crowded restaurant. "I can do better than that. When we came in I saw reservations for Rose on the list. I'll see if we can join her for coffee, providing it's all right with whomever she's dining."

She gave a wry look. "This wouldn't be a favor, would it?"

Mayor Roberts chuckled. "I see no reason to call it that.

It might be handy for me to have a direct link to the boys in Washington in my town." He winked. "Just in case something comes up that we can't handle by ourselves in town hall."

Their entrées arrived and they discussed Beth's proposal, agreeing there was a definite advantage to having the Congresswoman base her office in Bridgewater. After finishing, Mayor Roberts dabbed at his chin with his napkin and said. "Let's get this show on the road. I've given Rose enough time to eat and schmooze." He rose from his chair. "I think you might have something in common to use as a basis to begin chatting. Let me check it out first."

"That will give me time to call the office," Beth said sliding out from her chair. "I'll wait for you in the lobby." She tilted her head and shook her finger playfully in the air. "No favors promised here, right?"

The mayor shook his head. "Let's say that the possibilities for both sides are favorable and everything cancels out."

If Beth's eyes weren't playing tricks on her, Kent McReynolds was waiting to use the pay telephone near the coat room. She walked over and tapped him on the shoulder. "Are you following me?"

When Kent spun around, his eyes brightened. "Nice coincidence." He looked past her. "Are you alone, or is there a young, dashing business executive waiting to sprint you off for an afternoon rendezvous?"

"Just finishing a business lunch. I'm trying to nail down a promotion, so I'm following a hunch. The mayor I was dining with is trying to arrange a meeting right now with a Congresswoman I need to see. She's having lunch with an associate, so I'm not sure it's going to happen."

Kent felt the color drain from his face. "That Congresswoman's name wouldn't happen to be Clancey, would it?"

"Yes it is." She looked at him from beneath lowered brows. "This Congresswoman of yours, the one you're worried about, it wouldn't be . . ."

"Rose Clancey, my lunch guest."

Beth breathed an exasperated sigh. "That's quite a coincidence."

"Looks like we have another problem." Kent reached out and placed his hand on her upper arm in an almost apologetic gesture. "Now what?"

Beth ran through a series of short, disconnected thoughts as her mind reeled with a hundred possibilities, not all of them pleasant. "I'm not sure. This could get a little sticky." She felt Kent's fingers tense and realized the same thoughts were probably spinning through his mind as well.

Kent blew out a long breath. "We better start talking about our plans or nothing is going to work. Can we get together tonight?"

Beth shook her head. "It's going to be a late one at the office for me." When Kent's face looked disappointed, Beth quickly added, "but I can usually work and talk on the phone at the same time."

"I'll try to call," he said, just as Mayor Roberts came around the corner and signaled to Beth.

"Rose says she has about twenty minutes for us."

Beth nodded and tugged her hand away from Kent's. "Mayor Roberts, I'd like you to meet Captain McReynolds."

"Army?" the Mayor asked, extending his hand.

"No, Air Force, sir."

"What are you doing out of uniform, son?"

"I'm on leave, sir."

"That explains it. No military man on leave is ever caught dead in his uniform if he can help it. I was a

Marine, myself. Proud of it, too." The Mayor stepped
back. "But now, you'll have to excuse us. Miss Clarke
and I are joining an acquaintance of mine for some
coffee."

"The Congresswoman is my lunch guest, and I
would be pleased if you would allow me to buy you
that coffee."

All the way back to the table Kent's mind was in a
furious form of doublethink. On one side was the military. He didn't even have to think about how he felt
about the Air Force or about flying. It was instinct,
second nature, something that had been burned into
his character during his training and then had bonded
permanently and irrevocably.

On the other hand was Beth. He seemed to have
locked onto her the way his F-18 targeting computer
would lock onto an enemy mark. Being attracted to
her was an understatement and friendship wasn't
something he shared with women. But in this particular woman, he seemed to be able to find both. In this
case, it seemed that his own heart was close to taking
the hit—and he might very well take the Blue Eagle
down with him.

He forced himself back into focus, and reset the
relays inside his mind; even the one that kept tripping
back to Beth. As he tried to figure out how he was
going to maneuver his way around this situation, there
was one thing he knew for sure—all the Air Force
procedure manuals in the world couldn't help him. He
rolled his eyes to the ceiling and whispered a silent
prayer for mercy. This was going to be the longest
twenty minutes of his life.

As the trio approached the table, Beth was having
a little trouble of her own sorting through this new
dilemma. She had to forcibly remind herself that the

most important thing for the moment was not Kent McReynolds; it was Congresswoman Clancey.

Mayor Roberts eased Beth toward the Congresswoman. "Rose, I'd like you to meet Bethany Clarke. The firm she works for has brought a lot of opportunities to the town."

"I'm afraid that I put Mayor Roberts up to this, Madame Congresswoman," Beth said as polite formalities were exchanged. "I hope I'm not intruding."

Rose Clancey watched Kent return to his seat before glancing back at Beth. "Nonsense," she said, "Edward has filled me in on your plans for the office complex. I am interested." She scanned Beth's face as if deciding if a relationship with her would be beneficial. "Besides, from what Edward tells me, I think we have some other very interesting things in common."

Beth's nerves began twanging like a string on a toy guitar. "Similar interests? In Silvermeade?"

"In the Blue Eagles."

Beth glanced at Mayor Roberts. She had nearly forgotten that they had discussed the accident at length one day. And being friends with Rose Clancey, he would know about her fight in Congress. "I haven't thought about the Blue Eagles much lately," she said politely.

The Congresswoman sipped her coffee and eyed Kent's reaction. "Your face tells me otherwise. It's as transparent as a child's. That's refreshing in this day and age of cold career women."

Kent felt driven to come to Beth's rescue. "What Miss Clarke means is that she is not heavily involved in our little war, Madame Congresswoman."

A small twinge of indignation flared on Beth's face. "I can speak for myself, Captain McReynolds."

Kent nodded.

"I don't have a solid opinion on whether the Blue Eagles fly or not," she said, honestly.

The Congresswoman's lips pursed suspiciously. "But I know that Captain McReynolds does. I simply do not believe that the United States Air Force should be in show business."

Kent finished his coffee and wiped his mouth with the dark blue napkin. "It's not show biz at all. The entire performance is based strictly on maneuvers that any fighter pilot learns in the normal course of his training."

"That's technically true," Beth cut in, remembering vividly having the same argument with her brother many times, "but realistically, an Eagles show relates to training the same way television sitcoms portray real life."

"I don't agree, Miss Clarke," Kent cut in. "Doing those maneuvers help tighten and tone the concentration. The further on the edge, the higher the intensity."

"Captain McReynolds, I have no problem with intensity when it's necessary for combat and protecting this country," Beth said, blocking out that fact that she might be harming his cause for the moment. "But I do have a problem with putting our pilots in danger just for the sake of looking at life from upside down."

"I understand how you could feel that way," Kent quickly jumped back in, his voice crisp and clear, "but it does hone the senses. It also shows a pilot's abilities to the American people. We can't put our heads in the sand and ignore that fact either." His mission was to placate Congresswoman Clancey and convince her that the Air Force Demo team was good for American morale, and that's exactly what he was going to do— even if it meant stepping on Beth's beautiful toes.

He was about to say more when a voice came from

behind him. "As I live and breathe, it's Rose Clancey!"

The Congresswoman acknowledged her friend, and as she and Mayor Roberts turned away to strike up a conversation, Beth and Kent were left alone for the moment.

"Exactly what do you think you're doing?" Kent's voice was a whisper, but the uneasiness came through loud and clear.

"I'm just expressing my opinion."

"Express it later when we're alone. I'm losing points here." His brown eyes were flashing.

Beth rested an elbow on the table and set her chin in her hand. "You might be cute, but a flash of a smile or a wink of an eye is not about to change the way I feel."

Kent sat up straight and preened. "So, you think I'm cute?"

"Stop changing the subject."

"Answer the question."

"Stop it," she whispered as loudly as she could without attracting attention. "This is supposed to be a dignified business lunch."

"Answer the question and I'll go back to dignified." Kent turned his smile up a degree.

"Yes, you're cute," she admitted in an exasperated sigh.

"So are you."

Beth tightened her face into a disapproving look and then eased it into a smile as the Congresswoman returned her attention to Kent.

"Okay, so convince me, Captain," she said, not missing a beat in their conversation despite the interruption. She glanced at her watch. "You have fifteen minutes to convince me not to send the letters out to the Appropriations Committee until I can dig a little deeper into all this jet glitz."

"Fifteen minutes is hardly long enough to even begin."

"Put it in a nutshell for me, Captain."

Kent quickly organized his thoughts. "Well," he began, "the Blue Eagles play most of their dates at military installations and are booked for air shows by an office of the Department of Defense. Of course, for a modest fee, private air shows can also book the team." He noticed the look on the Congresswoman's face turn to skepticism. He held up a hand in a sign of caution. "Now I know what you're thinking, but we really do come cheap. With the team members getting about forty grand a year, the whole operation is budgeted for only two million annually."

"And what do we get for that bargain price, Captain?" the Congresswoman asked innocuously.

"In two thousand shows over the past thirty-four years, the Blue Eagles have been seen by a quarter of a billion people—more than any other team. We talk to anyone who wants to listen, shake hands, kiss babies, sign autographs, visit the sick . . ."

Unaffected by his spiel, the Congresswoman shook her head disapprovingly. "You see, it's just as I said. All show."

Okay, Kent thought, *move in another direction.* "And as I said, the maneuvers . . ."

"Stunts," Congresswoman Clancey corrected. "Don't you agree Beth?"

"I'm not sure," Beth answered, surprised that the Congresswoman had asked her. She was not about to lie, but neither did she want to shoot Kent's speech entirely full of holes. "But it all began in the late forties to hype reenlistments, isn't that right, Captain?"

"No, that was the Navy, Miss Clarke," Kent corrected.

"But even you have to admit that no matter which branch of the military does air shows, it's still stunts," Rose pressed.

"No, ma'am. They're maneuvers; maneuvers learned and practiced by every fighter pilot in flight service. Barrel rolls, pitch ups, delta rolls, they're all defensive moves. The skill of our pilots is our key to our deterrent position as a world leader." Kent's face came alive, his eyes burning brilliantly with conviction. "Just wait until one of us throws a clover loop at those troublemakers in the Gulf." He raised his hands, positioning one slightly in front of the other before circling them in the air. "Pow! All we'll see then is the back end of one of those Russian-made MIGs as it bugs out and heads for home!"

An expression of smug triumph spread over the Congresswoman's face. "It would seem then, by your own admission Captain, you Blue Eagles are practicing for something that is not ever supposed to happen because of our nation's reputation."

She's a cool one, he thought, *but I'm ready for her.* "Ma'am, it's hard to explain." His features fell into a meditative state and his voice became tinged with reserve. "You never want a war to happen, but you always wonder just how good you are. Could you protect yourself, your wingman and your country just as you were trained to do? Doing these . . ." he paused, waiting until he was sure all eyes were on him. ". . . maneuvers keeps you on the edge."

"There are other ways to stay on the edge, Captain," the Congresswoman challenged. "Reflexes can't be forced by putting pilots into impossible situations. They must come naturally to be effective."

Beth was becoming increasingly uncomfortable.

She only half-listened as she struggled with her con-
science; should she step in or let Kent battle this on
his own? No, she had to say something. "Madame
Congresswoman, much of what Captain McReynolds
is saying is true. The maneuvers *do* keep the pilots
sharp." Beth glanced at Kent. He was smiling encour-
agingly at her. "The one question my brother said he
was asked the most at appearances, was 'Is it all done
by computer?' With all the modern technology and
special effects in the movies, people are afraid to believe that real people can do such things. But the Eagle
pilots can do it all, and do it all manually."

Unaffected, the Congresswoman sought to throw
some additional fuel into the fire. "You're pretty quiet,
Edward. What do you think?"

Awkwardly he cleared his throat. "Being a Marine,
I think I'd side with the Captain here." He sipped his
coffee stirred it and sipped it again. "The planes are
not just for show. They could get dressed for war in
no time. Isn't that right, son?"

"Yes, sir. If a war did happen, it would only take
three days to paint camouflage on the red white and
black F-18s, and replace the show smoke canisters
with guns. And because we, the present team, and the
Eagle pilots who have toured before us were practicing
all this time to be the best, we would be."

"Maybe, but I would hope that our fighter pilots
wouldn't need stunt flying to stay sharp," Congresswoman Clancey said, not willing to concede the point.

Beth could not stand by and let the Congresswoman
bury Kent completely. "But you have to admit that all
that flying couldn't hurt either," she quickly put in.

Kent's face brightened. "I think we can all agree on
that point." *Thank you Beth,* he thought.

Congresswoman Clancey was clearly enjoying the
battle. "I've heard all the PR before. I've read it in

your pamphlets. Now I want to know what the pilot thinks. Why *are* you up there dodging clouds, Captain McReynolds?"

"It's a mission and it's a love." Kent could not have been more honest. "The loops and rolls, all of it, is daring and fun, but it can't compare to the first moment that you level off. The whole sky is above you, visible though the clear canopy."

The Congresswoman offered only a distracted nod in return. "Nothing different than what I see out of the window of a commercial airliner."

"Completely different," Kent corrected quickly. "The way you're seated in the cockpit of an F-18, you can't see the plane's wings. It's just you and the sky. You are Icarus and you're flying the sky."

Congresswoman Clancey smiled wickedly. "So, it's really more of an adventure experience for the pilots rather than a military exercise, isn't it?"

"Quite the opposite," Kent replied. "It's skill and pride. Up there the plane becomes part of you. The stick is an extension of your arm. Your body must be in top physical shape to endure up to eight and a half times its own weight in pressure." He began to gesture with his hands while he spoke. It was the only way he knew how to emphasize what had to be understood in order to be fully appreciated. "Ma'am, there is no cruise control up there. Just to stay level, a pilot must apply twelve pounds of pressure to the stick at all times, flying at what we call 'full nose down trim'. That takes practice, confidence and concentration. Mental intensity is part of flying the diamond, the same mental intensity that is needed for combat."

Beth was totally taken aback by the sparkle in Kent's eyes. He truly believed in everything that he was saying, and it showed on his face. Although she'd heard it many times before from her brother, even she was becoming mesmerized by the aerial ballet Kent was painting inside her head.

Kent took additional charge with quiet, but firm, assurances. "Ma'am, we don't fly by computer; we fly by skill and instinct. For example, when the solos pass each other exactly at show center, they have no idea how they look to the crowd. All they have is their own satisfaction of doing well. If one miscalculates by even a fraction of a second, the pass can be off hit by as much as four hundred feet!"

Congresswoman Clancey leaned forward on one elbow and set her chin in her palm. She drew her brows together thoughtfully. "Interesting. I never really thought much about that angle, Captain. But that doesn't mean I'm ready to whistle 'The Wild Blue Yonder' just yet."

But she would be soon, Kent vowed silently. There was just one more pitch to make. "More important than all the technical stuff are the people who come out to see us. They don't come out to root against the Blue Eagles. Heck, we're the good guys."

A smile curled up on the Congresswoman's lips. "Just who are you trying to convince, Captain? Me or Miss Clarke?"

Kent hadn't realized it, but for most of the time he was talking, he had been looking into Beth's eyes. And for a brief moment before the Congresswoman spoke, he thought he saw something new there.

He turned his own smile up a notch to match the Congresswoman's as he turned toward her. "Why you, of course, Madame Congresswoman. I want you to put away the paring knife when it comes to our budget."

"Captain, I must admit, you're good. Very good." Congresswoman Clancey touched her head in a mock salute. "Have you ever considered going into politics after your tour with the Air Force is over?"

Kent's grin flashed wide for a brief instant and then relaxed into a smaller friendly smile. "No, ma'am. I'm afraid I'm a career man."

"Too bad. You'd be a natural." She looked down at her watch. "I'd like to continue our talk, but if I don't leave now I'll be late for my meeting with the Governor."

"Was I convincing enough for you, Madame Congresswoman?" Kent said beaming, sure he had made some progress.

"Not bad, but I still have my reservations."

Kent hesitated, trying to decide if he should continue his attack. "I know that you'll read about the accidents of the early squads, so if you will allow me, I'd like to have the reports sent to you."

"You do cut right to the chase, don't you?"

"Yes, ma'am. I figure since your first thought was to cut our budget, you would be digging into our past to use whatever ammo you could find. My job is to neutralize some of the explosion if I can."

"You're right," the Congresswoman replied. "Since you've put all your cards on the table, I will too. I am going to dig deep to see what I come up with. Then we'll see."

"Yes ma'am," Kent agreed, feeling that he had already succeeded in mellowing some of her hostility. "I think you will."

A few people stopped Mayor Roberts and the Congresswoman on their way out, while Beth and Kent continued on to the foyer.

"Can I drop you off somewhere?" He took a step closer to her.

"No, thanks." Even after the intensity of the meeting with the Congresswoman, she found the urge to step into his arms almost too strong to ignore. But somehow it didn't happen. "I'm sorry if I put you on the spot, but I do need that contact."

"And I have a job to do, myself, so I couldn't let you get away with too much either."

"This is really getting complicated, isn't it?"

"What if I promise to try to keep it simple from now on?"

"Simple?" Beth's laugh sounded more like a sigh. "Kent, you know as well as I do that when it comes to the military, nothing is ever simple."

Chapter Seven

It was only six o'clock. Kent knew Beth wouldn't be home yet. He walked to the front of the old farmhouse, sat down on the porch swing and pushed back with the tip of one shoe, starting the swing into a lazy motion. The hypnotic creak of the rusted chain sent his thoughts drifting.

He hated self-confessions, but he had a pretty good idea what was happening. The same attraction he felt the first day he laid eyes on Beth was back. The same feelings he had that night years ago at the Flight Line Bar and Grill when he kissed her were fighting with his commitment to his mission.

He could honestly say he'd never been in love before. Sure, he had stretches during which he dated just one woman, but it wasn't love. This was different. He could feel it.

But he also knew the problems that stood between them. Could he convince her it was time to trust enough to open up her heart and let him in? Could he balance his love of the sky and her fear of it, and make her feel secure when he walked out the door to the flight line every day? The answers seemed as overwhelming as the questions.

The creek of a door cut into his thoughts, as Gerry pushed open the front door with her hip. She smiled, offering Kent one of the two steaming mugs of coffee she carried. "I thought you might like some company while you waited for Bethie."

"Thank you. I'd like that, ma'am," Kent said, stopping the motion of the swing and rising to his feet.

"She should be home soon," Gerry said.

"Yes, ma'am." Kent steadied the swing with his free hand and waited until Gerry sat down before joining her.

Gerry put the swing back into gentle motion with a light push. "Please, stop calling me ma'am. It makes me feel like my own grandmother. Call me Gerry or Mrs. Carter."

"Yes, ma'am . . . er, Mrs. Carter."

For a few minutes they sat in silence, watching the breeze send yellow clouds of dust across the newly plowed field opposite the farmhouse. To their left, cows lumbered back toward the barn for evening milking and a tractor headed for home. "I like it out here this time of day. It's quiet. Gives you time to think," Gerry said, raising the mug to her lips. She sipped the coffee and peered over the rim, measuring Kent with wise, blue eyes.

Kent arched his arm across the back of the swing. "I've been thinking a bit."

"About Beth?" Gerry smiled when Kent nodded. She took another small sip of tea. "Do you like her?"

"Yes, I do."

"A lot?"

"Ma'am?"

Gerry gave Kent's knee a motherly pat. "Relax, this isn't a military inquiry. I'm just curious."

"Yes, a lot."

"Then you'll be staying around for a while?"

He raised an eyebrow. "Not for very long, I'm afraid. The Blue Eagles are playing an air show at McGuire Air Force Base in south Jersey in two weeks. Hopefully by then I'll know where I stand with my mission here. Then it's back home to Nellis for a week before leaving for a show in Hawaii."

Gerry sighed. "Oh my. That isn't very much time, is it?"

"No, I'm afraid it isn't."

Gerry placed her coffee mug in her lap. She gave him a sad smile. "You didn't get to know Steven very well, did you?"

"Colonel Clarke and I were just getting to know each other when the accident happened."

"And David?"

"I didn't know him as well as I would have liked, I'm afraid. The solos usually practice alone without the diamond until it's time to do a show drill. But we all felt the void when the team was lost." The old feelings were welling up in his throat, the memories causing a hard lump to build in his chest. Fortunately, as he sipped his coffee, he managed to swallow the guilt that usually came with the sadness.

Gerry stopped the swing and put her empty cup down. "It must be very hard for you sometimes. I'll never forget when you came to the house right after the memorial service. It was your eyes I first noticed that day. They were so sad, so full of pain. I knew that I would never forget them."

Kent hunched over and set his mug on the porch

floor. He rested his forearms on his thighs. "It was a tragic loss."

"Yes dear, it was. And it was a real blow to Beth."

There was a long, brittle silence during which Kent felt every muscle in his body harden. He could feel his natural defense closing his throat as he tried to speak.

Gerry watched Kent's expression grow somber during their conversation. She reached out and touched his hand with a few caring pats. "Want to tell me about it?"

Kent straightened, his eyes coming up to lock onto Gerry's. It was a full five seconds before he finally said, "Yes, ma'am, I believe that I would."

As Beth eased the car into the driveway, she could plainly see two figures swaying on her aunt's front porch swing. She looked at her watch, and wondered just how long her aunt had been chewing on Kent's ear.

"What are you two plotting?" she asked as she got out of the car.

Kent got to his feet and helped Gerry from the swing. "Nothing. Your aunt was just keeping me company."

"I couldn't let him sit out here all alone," Gerry said, picking up her mug from the table. Taking Kent's mug from the floor, she walked to the front door. "I'll just be getting these dishes washed now." She turned back to Kent. "I'm very glad we had this time to talk."

"I am too. Thank you, Mrs. Carter."

"What talk?" Beth asked, with a smile of warning to her aunt.

"Never you mind," Gerry replied, allowing Kent to hold open the front door for her, "if you need to know, you'll know." She winked up at Kent before disappearing inside.

"I think I'm in trouble," Beth said as she and Kent walked back to her apartment door.

"Your aunt and I were getting to know each other better."

Beth laughed. "No one ever gets to know Aunt Gerry. She's constant change and stoic resistance all rolled up into one." She took two steps up and sat on a chair on the smaller rear porch.

Kent rubbed the back of his neck and leaned against a wooden post. "I think we need to talk."

"About the Congresswoman?"

"For one thing."

"Want to come up?"

Kent looked toward the western sky. "Doesn't look like rain. How about a walk instead?"

Beth couldn't help noticing that when Kent smiled, tiny laugh lines fanned out from his eyes that made him look a little like Harrison Ford. She guessed that in a few hundred years from now, someone like Kent would be shooting around the stars in a spacecraft instead of shooting around the clouds in a jet. And someone like her would probably be trying to talk herself out of getting close to him because of it.

A man like Kent was like a butterfly. You could catch him and pin him down, but then he wouldn't be a butterfly anymore. Kent belonged to the sky. A man like him could never be talked out of his dreams. Steven couldn't be. David couldn't be. And Kent wouldn't be, either. That's why she would have to step back and let him continue to reach out and touch the sky. Alone. Without restrictions. Without promises that could never be kept.

"I suppose a little jog wouldn't hurt either one of us," Beth said, recovering from her reverie and giving

Kent a playful pat on his stomach. "We have been eating a lot lately, and those flight suits are form-fitting. Wait here, it will just take me a minute to change."

She reappeared in snug-fitting jeans and an old New York Mets batting jersey. Kent grinned openly when he saw her. "I thought we were going for a walk, not to shag some fly balls. Besides, I'm a Dodgers fan."

"Not around here, you're not," she replied, already a few steps ahead of him in the driveway. "When my Uncle Joe gets back, you'd better be able to recite the Mets starting line-up, complete with batting average and uniform number, from memory."

They started down a dirt road that wound its way past the farmhouse. About a mile down, the road turned toward the river. Along the way Beth pointed out important local sights, such as the herd of cows grazing on Beekman Farms and the endless stretch of Duke's Estate, with its hundreds of deer protected and fed by the millionaire heiress' will.

Kent looked over at Beth as she spoke. A year ago he would have laughed if someone told him that sharing such a simple thing as a walk in the country with a woman would be as meaningful to him as chasing sunsets in his F-18, but it was. Being with Beth, talking to her, the casual caresses of their hands as they walked together was as exciting to him as revving up the jet engines in his plane and listening to the roar that begged him to soar into the twilight.

At the end of the road, he helped her over the barrier used to keep cars out of the river bed. A few hundred feet farther and the grass disappeared, giving way to moss, river silt and huge rocks which formed a small waterfall.

"It's nice here," Kent said, listening to the soft rush

of the running river and the occasional call of a bird. "It's peaceful."

"I come here to think," Beth said, stepping up onto some of the large rocks. "The sound of rippling water clears my head." She looked over at him and extended her hand. "You'd better come up here before you get swallowed up to your knees in the mud."

Kent glanced down at his sneakers. They were already half buried in brown muck and sinking fast. "Move over." he said.

At the touch of Kent's hand, a pleasant sensation of warmth momentarily distracted her. "I think this is a good place to clear the air," she said with a nervous flutter in her stomach.

Kent found some small rocks and threw them into the water as he talked. "Your brother was quite a man, Beth. Although I only knew him for a short while, I'll never forget him."

"I thought we came here to talk about the Congress-woman."

"We will."

Beth cast her eyes downward to hide whatever emotions might be mirrored there. "What about David? Did you know him well?" She didn't need to look at Kent to know he was staring at her.

"No, not really," he said, his voice low and composed. "I was only at Nellis for a few weeks when—" He stopped. Some wounds scar, some stay open forever. "They were both exceptional people."

Beth sighed. "Yes, they were."

"And you are too."

Beth lifted her head. "You still hardly know me."

Kent reached out and brushed a stray lock of hair from her eyes. "Oh, you'd be surprised just how much I know. Besides being beautiful on the outside, you're beautiful inside, too. You're strong enough to have taken what happened to you and built upon it. You didn't hide, you went on. Colonel Clarke would have been proud of you." He tripped over his next words. "Captain Mays, too."

When Beth spoke, her voice wavered. "I'd trade that compliment for one of those good old fashioned arguments Steven and I used to have about flying." She felt tears building.

Kent wanted to hold her, but sensed it was not the time. He reached down and scooped up a few more stones. "I can tell by your job that you like to be challenged. But I also sense that in your rise to the top, you didn't climb over anyone to do it."

"I suppose I've bruised a few toes in the process."

"Something else I know, Miss Bethany Clarke, is that for now, we're going to do it your way." He stopped tossing pebbles into the water and looked into her eyes. "But I won't lie to you. I think I want more than that."

Beth had a wild urge to throw herself into his arms, but didn't. "Are you always this direct?"

"I try to be," he said as he tossed another stone into the center of the river.

"Good. Because I want a direct answer. Why do you fly?"

Kent shifted closer to her, set his right foot on a small rock and rested on his arm on his thigh. "I've been told that I had the itch to fly almost since birth."

"Let me guess. Your dad was a pilot."

"Right. Still wears his Air Force academy ring."

"So you followed in his footsteps."

"Family tradition."

Beth saw the wonder on Kent's face as he watched a large bird take off from the opposite bank and fly across the water. He followed its rise to the sky with his eyes, and she could tell that even after all the time he spent in the air, he was still awed by the sheer miracle of flight. Watching him in the dimming light, his faced seemed almost childlike in his genuine love of the heavens. When he turned back to face her, she could actually feel his dreams. His eyes sparkled as he continued.

"When I was a child playing with the other boys, they would get all excited when the train whistle would blow, and talk about going wherever it was that the train was going."

"But not you."

"Nope. I'd look up and watch for planes. I didn't care where they were going, I just wanted to be up there with them".

"And the little boy followed his dream right into the sky," Beth said, feeling a warm glow flow though her, cracking her resolve as his happiness spread out to her. "Now it's your life."

"So far. But lately, I've started to think that I need a center to that life. Maybe a happy forever-after with someone special to share it with."

"Right now forever to me is just a long weekend."

"How long can you be satisfied with a bunch of weekends?"

Beth shrugged. "It'll do for a while." She picked up a small rock and tossed it into the water, watching it land about four feet out. "You seem to have managed to stay unattached. A bachelor Blue Eagle is as rare as hen's teeth."

"I just haven't met anyone special."

"You have hundreds of people falling in love with you at every air show. Surely one of them came close."

"I've dated. Some. But nothing serious or long term."

Beth folded her arms across her chest and looked him straight in the eye. "I know the shtick. The Air Force wants a homey image for its stars. No mustaches, no long hair, no frequenting bars after nine P.M. if you're wearing identifying markings. How did you get onto the team, anyway?"

Kent grinned and raked a hand through his sandy hair. "Talent, darlin', pure talent."

"In or out of the sky?"

"Both. You know very well that the pilots are chosen, flying skills notwithstanding, for PR qualities. Legend has it that no Blue Eagle before me," he winked, "nor any to come after, will be able to beat me at public speaking." He turned his grin up. "Or at golf. Playing eighteen holes with movers and shakers helps the Blue Eagles survive."

"PR, huh? Some of which, I see, you are trying out on me. Unsuccessfully, I might add." She looked up at the darkening sky. "I guess we should head back to the house before the night creatures come out." A wide grin broke open onto her face. "But I suppose, with your garrulous, thumbs-up attitude, you could talk any bear out of his dinner, couldn't you?"

He stood and dusted off the seat of his jeans with one hand. "The only wild animal within miles is that old cow we saw in the last field, so I think we're safe." He stepped down from their perch and held out his hand to Beth.

As she stood, she lost her footing on a wet rock and nearly tumbled down the bank. Kent was right there, blocking her fall and catching her in his outstretched arms. What happened next certainly wasn't planned. But with Beth now resting against his chest, with his lips hovering just above hers, it was the natural thing to do. He set her back on her feet, wound his fingers in her hair and kissed her.

"More PR?" she murmured when they drew apart again.

"Hardly. This is strictly personal."

Chapter Eight

On the way back to the farmhouse it was hard for Beth to control the warning voice inside her head. She might be out of practice, but she wasn't naive. She knew what was happening to her. He had said she was strong, but he was wrong. She was ill-equipped to fight the fact that she wanted be with this tall sandy-haired man who had come quietly into her life and breathed new vitality into a dying heart. There was just that little, miserable part of her mind that knew they could never have the forever he wanted.

At the back stairs to her apartment Kent turned and put his hands on her shoulders. He slid one hand down her left arm to her wrist and with the other lifted her chin to tilt her face to his. "What about us?"

He watched as Beth pressed her lips together and he saw a flush spread from her cheeks to her neck. "We don't have to talk about it, if it makes you uncomfortable," he said in a whisper against her cheek. "I'll understand."

"Shut up and kiss me," Beth said.

When they parted, Kent ran his forefinger along her forehead, down her nose to its tip. "You're trembling. Are you okay?"

"I think so." She was surprised to hear Kent's words echo her own thoughts. "How about you?"

Tell her, you jerk, his mind screamed. Tell her that you're falling in love with her and, while you're at it, tell her all that other stuff you've been rehearsing. But "I'm fine," was all that was able to come out of his mouth.

"Consequences," she said with a sigh.

Kent threw an arm over his head. "You too? I was thinking the same thing."

"The last time I fell in . . ." she stopped and bit her lower lip, ". . . I got involved with a pilot, I lost him."

He understood her fear. "Do you believe in destiny?"

Beth closed her eyes and thought about her answer. "I believe in fate, in God, and maybe even in miracles," she said softly. "But maybe not in the future."

"The future will give us everything if you'll only let it."

It was 11:30 PM and *Nightline* was coming on. Gerry had heard Beth and Kent's voices earlier and knew they had gone around to the back porch. She sipped her chamomile tea and smiled just as she heard a car door slam. The sound of footsteps on the front porch told her that her husband was home. She set aside her thoughts of Beth for the time being.

"Joseph, is that you?"

"Who else would it be at this hour?" A large man of about sixty with silver hair and warm brown eyes set two suitcases down next to the sofa before pecking a quick kiss on Gerry's cheek. "Whose car is that in the driveway?" He glanced quickly around the room, looking for his wife's late night visitor.

"A friend of Bethie's."

"The car's got a rental sticker on it," Joe said walking down the hall to their bedroom.

Gerry went into the kitchen and put her teacup in the sink. She walked back into the living room and turned off the TV set before following her husband to their room. "You must be tired after your trip. We'll talk in the morning."

Joe straightened from the dresser drawer he had been digging inside and frowned. "Geraldine, what is going on here? Any other day you'd give me their name, address, next of kin, and heaven-only-knows-what else." His eyes narrowed. "Beth's friend wouldn't be a man, would it?"

"Maybe."

"How long has she known him?"

"That's a bit hard to say with this young man."

The corner of Joe's mouth twitched in exasperation. "If you ask me, Beth doesn't need any problems right now."

Gerry shook her finger in Joe's direction, "No one's asking you, so never you mind. Besides, I approve of this young man."

Joe sat on the bed and removed his shoes as he spoke. "I've only been gone two weeks. It's too quick." He tossed them on the floor with a clunk. "Remember what happened with David?"

Gerry picked up the shoes and carried them to the closet, just like she had done for forty years. "Yes, but I think this could be different than what happened with David."

"Don't get me wrong, David was a fine man. I liked him."

"We all did, Joseph. He and our Steven were very close."

Joe peeled off his socks and tossed them onto the bedroom floor. "I still say he rushed Beth into making a commitment before she was ready."

"Now, dear," Gerry said, picking up the socks and tossing them into the laundry hamper next to the closet, "we don't know that for sure."

"The heck we don't. The poor girl had Steven telling her how much David loved her and how great it would be to have another pilot in the family. She had it all built up in her mind before she even got a chance to see if it was real or not. That's why she took it so hard when he died. She hurt, no doubt about that, but she didn't hurt like someone really in love, and she knew it. I tell you, that's the reason she keeps putting off finding someone else and starting a family." He looked toward the back of the farmhouse.

Gerry gave him a firm pat on his shoulder. "Joseph, our Beth is a good girl."

"I know that, but what about him?"

Pretending she didn't hear, Gerry continued, "If something is starting between the two of them, it's because she is in love."

"Is she?" Joe pulled a pair of striped pajamas from the dresser before walking to their bathroom door and yanking it open. "Maybe, maybe not. I don't intend to let anyone rush her into anything again until she's ready."

Gerry waved him off as he turned the water on in the sink. "That's not for us to decide. Besides, nobody's rushing anybody."

Brushing his teeth, Joe mumbled something incoherent before sticking his head back out the door.

"First thing in the morning, I'm going to have a talk with her." He waved the toothbrush in the air, splashing the mirror with water. "And the next time that young man comes around, him too."

"Nonsense," Gerry said, wiping droplets from the mirror. "You'll do no such thing. There's no point in getting all upset about something you can't do anything about anyway. Love is love and it happens when it darn well pleases."

"Humph!" Joseph mumbled in protest, brushing his teeth with a fierce, angry motion.

A gentle knock at the door pulled Beth from her sleep. "Just a minute," she called out. She remembered her walk with Kent and smiled. "I'll be right there."

As she dressed, she thought about Kent. No strings, no attachments. When the time came he would go from her life just as quietly as he had come into it. It was simple, wasn't it? She pursed her lips together to keep them from quivering. If she was hurt, it was no one's fault but her own.

She opened the door. It was Kent. "Hey there! You're supposed to wake up smiling. I did!" Kent walked in carrying two cups of coffee from Starbucks.

"I didn't think I would see you again so soon."

Kent tucked a wayward strand of hair behind her ear. "I hope that you have a better opinion of me than that."

When he moved closer, she made sure she took a long drink of the hot liquid, ignoring the burn as it trailed down her throat. She was a mature woman, she was supposed to be able to handle situations like this. But it was hard to handle the way she was feeling about Kent. She looked at him, remembering how much fun they had shared. She wanted to be with him forever, but a critical voice cut into her thoughts.

He was too much like her brother and David. He had the same dreams, same visions, the same reckless abandon. Chasing sunsets for a living, cutting the sky like a razor blade and living on the edge were all that mattered to men like them. She wasn't sure love could ever replace that feeling.

"I just thought you'd be out doing things. After all, there's nothing worse than an out-of-work hero."

He laughed. "We heroes are never out of work, just resting until the next quest comes along."

His sparkling eyes distracted her. She had to move away from them. "I've got to call the office. Thanks to you, I'm going to be late."

"Another consequence," Kent said, winking. "Complaining?"

"No." She reached for the phone. "Commenting."

"Comment on this," he said, placing a kiss on her cheek.

Beth giggled as Annie answered on the other end of the line. "Hi. I'm going to be late." She paused. "About nine-thirty."

"Make it ten," Kent whispered playfully.

The smile on his face made it hard for her to refuse. "Make that ten," Beth agreed. With her eyes on his smile, she reached out to hang up the phone but instead sent the entire unit clanging onto the floor. "Annie probably heard that. I'm going to have some explaining to do."

Downstairs, Joe heard the clamor going on just over his head. He saw the car drive up and he didn't like it, didn't like it one bit. No matter what Gerry said, he was going to corner this 'friend' of Beth's and find out just what was going on with his niece. No one was going to hurt her again.

* * *

Beth had only been gone fifteen minutes, and already Kent missed her. *I must be going crazy,* he decided after finishing with the call he made to Colonel Eagle. *Nope, it was definitely love.* He angled his watch to his eyes. In about eight hours Beth would be back and he'd tell her so. For sure this time.

But for now, he had a job to do and he'd better get started. First to the recruiting station to do a little recruiting of his own. Sergeant Lowry was about to become an official, if temporary, member of the Blue Eagles for a promotional hospital tour.

Kent bounced down the back steps, whistling and taking two stairs at a time. But his elation turned to caution as soon as he pushed open the back door. There, with a cross look on his face and arms folded across his chest, Joe leaned against the big oak tree facing Beth's apartment.

Half in anticipation, half in dread, he walked right over and extended his hand. "Mr. Carter. Nice to see you again." They had a lot of contact with each other during the memorial service at Nellis.

Slowly Joe unfolded his arms, his eyes never leaving Kent's. The handshake was firm and tight. "Lieutenant McReynolds. What on earth are you doing here?"

Their eyes held, studying each other freely. "It's Captain now, sir. I'm on temporary assignment."

"What does that have to do with my niece?"

"Nothing," Kent said in a voice filled with both honesty and respect as he looked the older man right in the eye, "and everything, sir. I think I'm in love with her."

Joe's expression was like a stone mask. "You *think* you're in love with her? Heck, son, I may be old-fashioned, but in this family, after what my wife has told me about this whirlwind romance, you'd better do more than *think* you love her."

Kent ran a hand through his hair, stalling for time. He wanted to make sure that what he told Joe didn't sound like a lie. After all, before he met Beth, if someone would have told him that you could get to know a woman and fall in love with her in just two short weeks, he wouldn't have believed it either. Still, it had happened. "No, sir. I mean, yes sir. I *am* in love with Beth."

The snappy eyes that looked out from Joe's time-toughened face showed plainly that the man wasn't convinced. He walked over and threw an arm around Kent's shoulders. "Son, do you know what you need?"

"No, sir."

"A hot cup of Geraldine's morning coffee."

"Now?" Kent asked.

Joe's face became sober. "Yes. Right now."

Chapter Nine

"I heard two voices before you hung up, one of them distinctly male," Annie said, following Beth close enough to qualify as her shadow.

Beth wiped a silver teaspoon with a blue linen napkin. "I can't talk about this now. Congresswoman Clancey will be here any second."

"She can wait. I can't. Is he gorgeous, or what?"

As Kent's face focused in her mind, Beth agreed. "Very attractive." She let a slight smile cross her face before snapping it off. "But there's more to him than just good looks."

"Such as?"

"Honesty, warmth, strength, intelligence, sensitivity."

Annie reached down and pulled the strap of her left shoe back up over her heel. "Sounds about as all-American as fast food." She looked Beth squarely in the eye. "What's the catch?"

Beth fastidiously checked the rest of the silverware for spots and carefully avoided Annie's eyes. "It's nothing."

"C'mon, we have no secrets. What's the problem with this guy? Serial killer? Political terrorist?"

Beth gave a weary sigh as she sat down in one of the chairs. "He's more All-American than you think. He's Air Force."

"No!" Annie rolled out the word. "You're kidding. I can't believe you've fallen for another pilot!"

With vulnerable eyes, Beth stared at her friend. "Worse. I've fallen for another Blue Eagle."

Back at the farmhouse, Joe had Kent cornered in the kitchen. "Okay, so I'll give you that much; you say you care for Beth. But so did Dave Mays."

Kent gulped down a large swallow of coffee. "Yes sir, I'm sure he did. And I'm sure Beth loved Captain Mays, too."

Joe set his coffee mug down on the print tablecloth and signaled to Gerry for a refill. "Well, I don't know about that."

Kent swallowed his astonishment with another big slug of coffee. Caution made his heart pound a furious rhythm in his chest. Beth didn't seem to him like the type of woman who would agree to spend the rest of her life with a man she didn't love. "They were engaged."

Over Joe's left shoulder, Gerry poured fresh coffee into his mug. "David was Steven's closest friend, you know." She moved next to Kent but he covered his cup with his hand, declining the refill. "They had gone to the Academy together, and through a series of transfers they wound up flying together."

"How did he meet Beth?" Kent asked as casually as he could over his racing heart.

Gerry sat down across from her husband. "Gayle, Steven's wife, invited Beth out to spend the holidays with them." She noticed that Joe was glaring at her. She put a hand to her lips. "I'm sorry, dear. This was your story, wasn't it."

Joe waved at her to continue. "Go ahead. You'll only cut in sooner or later anyway."

Dismissing him with a curt toss of her head, Gerry turned to Kent. "David fell head over heels in love with our Beth the moment he saw her, or so Gayle said in her letters. He started coming over to Steven and Gayle's house every day, and before you knew it, he and Bethie were getting married."

"Too fast," Joe mumbled.

Gerry gave Joe a warning look. "Hush, let me finish." She turned back to Kent. "Anyway, they spent every possible minute together right up until, well, you know the rest, Kent."

Awkwardly Kent cleared his throat. "Perhaps I should wait until Beth's ready to tell me this."

"I don't know if she can." Gerry said. "I'm not convinced she knows one way or the other if she really loved David."

Joe leaned his elbows onto the table. "David was Steve's age, thirty-eight." He rubbed his chin with his hand. "Made him, oh, ten, eleven years older than Beth. She was still working on her Masters. She was young, bright, but awfully naive about certain things. Went out there and *wham*," he slammed his hand down on the kitchen table, making even Gerry jump, "walked right into a double team. I think Steven liked the idea of his best friend being part of the family."

"So what you're saying is that perhaps Beth only agreed to marry Captain Mays to please her brother?"

Joe leaned back and folded his arms across his chest. "What I'm saying is that I think Beth convinced herself that David was the guy for her before she had a chance to find out. Steven talked it up until it became as real to her as it could be in such a short time." He shifted in the chair and tapped a finger on his coffee mug. "But when he was gone, the pain she went through was very real. Nearly tore her apart."

Kent looked down at his coffee and then up at Joe. "And you think I may be rushing her, too."

"It's too fast in my mind."

Gerry put a hand to her chest and looked at Joe with wistful eyes. "Aren't whirlwind romances wonderful?"

"Geraldine, stop distracting me."

Gerry gave Kent a conspiratorial wink and he relaxed a little. At least he seemed to have *one* ally.

"I'm only saying that real love at first sight *is* possible," she said, determined to get her point across before Joe scared Kent off completely. She reached out and patted her husband's hand. "Why, the moment you laid eyes on me you followed me around like a puppy until you caught me."

Joe reddened. "Okay, so maybe it is possible. But what I'm trying to get at, in a roundabout way, is that I won't stand by and let someone push Beth into something a second time."

"Sir, I wouldn't do something like that to Beth."

Joe's eyes scalded Kent when he spoke. "Heck son, if you ask me, it seems as though you're well on your way."

Gerry walked back to the stove. "Remember, dear, no one asked you."

"Sir, I assure you, I would not do that."

"Gerry tells me you're flying outta here in a few weeks. Where will that leave her then?"

Kent took charge of the conversation with quiet assurance. "Mr. Carter, I love your niece, and I want her in my life. I think she feels the same for me, and I hope that by the time I have to leave, Beth will tell me her feelings so we can decide what to do together. If she can't, I won't force the issue. I promise you that, sir." Kent's own words nearly choked him with the possibility that he would have to leave Beth behind. That thought was beginning to become more frightening than crashing a jet ever was.

"And right through this skyway, will be the Silvermeade Hotel," Beth said as she stood in the center of the walkway with Annie and Congresswoman Clancey. "Luxury accommodations for about a thousand guests with everything at their fingertips, including a staff that will cater to their every whim."

Rose Clancey nodded. "I have a few more questions before I sit down and hash out this idea with my staff."

"Any questions I can't answer, Annie will research and get back to you with tomorrow." Beth extended her arm and motioned for the Congresswoman to accompany her back to her office as Annie scribbled notes on a yellow legal pad.

They walked in silence for a few steps before Congresswoman Clancey abruptly said, "So, Miss Clarke, your older brother and fiancé were killed in the Blue Eagle crash at Indian Springs."

The Congresswoman's voice was as cold as ice, and it made Beth shiver. "It was a tragic accident."

"And an unnecessary one. The Air Force has been lucky since then, but it's only a matter of time."

"Not necessarily. No Blue Eagle show has ever been scrubbed for maintenance reasons, Madame Congresswoman. My brother used to say that his crew chief was better at maintaining the jet than he was at flying it." *Don't do it* Beth screamed inside her head, *don't ask me to get involved in your side of the argument.*

Congresswoman Clancy stopped at the elevators. "You can tell me the truth, Miss Clarke. That handsome pilot isn't here now. How do you really feel about the Blue Eagle program?"

Beth touched Annie's elbow. "Could you run up to legal and get the Congresswoman a copy of our standard lease?" She waited until Annie left on the elevator before continuing. "Is that one of the additional questions you had about the tower lease?"

"No, I'm just curious."

"I have no definite feelings one way or the other."

"I'm surprised."

"Whether or not the Blue Eagles continue to perform is a government matter best decided by those we elect."

"You would trust that decision to someone like me, then?"

"Yes I would, Madame Congresswoman. I have every confidence in your ability to do your job." Beth rang for the elevator. "And it's my place to try and convince you that the perfect place for that job would be here at Silvermeade."

"How do you plan to do that, Miss Clarke?"

"It all starts with a reception held in your honor so you can experience our service." She felt threatened, but brushed the feeling away and focused on her goal. "And I'm sure that how I feel about the Blue Eagles won't enter into your decision."

"I'll tell you how *I* feel about those throttle jockeys."

It was Alex Kirkland's voice. Beth was irritated to see him only a step or two away from the elevator doors just as Annie emerged with the contract. "Annie, why don't you take the Congresswoman to my office. I'll be up shortly and we can discuss the guest list for the reception."

Beth made sure the elevator doors were safely closed before spinning on her heels to face Alex. "How long have you been lurking around the halls eavesdropping on our conversation?"

Kirkland feigned sensitivity. "I'm shocked you'd accuse me of that."

"I call it as I see it!"

"Is the reception for everyone, or just a chosen few?"

"Everyone involved in planning the Development will be invited. Even you." Her blue eyes narrowed in suspicion and dislike. "But I warn you, Alex, if you do anything at all to ruin this for me. . . ."

He cut her off mid-sentence. "Relax. I'll only be there to tie up the loose ends when you admit that you can't pull this thing off all by yourself. I'll get Clancey's signature on the lease and—" he stopped, a devious smile crossing his lips, "*then* we'll see who becomes the next AVP."

"Don't bother, Alex. There are no loose ends in this deal," Beth said, snapping a smile of defiance onto her face. "The AVP position will go to the person who is best qualified." A wry glint came into her eyes. "And I do believe that will be me." She walked into the elevator without waiting for a reply and heard Alex muttering to himself as the door closed in his face.

Chapter Ten

Kent ran the razor over his chin, gathering a cloud of white foam beneath the blade. *Shoot,* he thought as he rinsed it underwater running from the faucet, *what on earth is wrong with me?* As he shaved his throat, he couldn't shake off the dark premonition that crept into his mind. He and Beth were on a collision course professionally and personally. He turned off the water and dried his face with a towel. He wanted too much. How on earth could he possibly have it all?

He put his hands on the rim of the sink and leaned forward. "In an hour you're meeting her for dinner," he said aloud to the stranger in the mirror. "What's the plan now, stud?"

It was much too late to change the way he felt and he knew it. But the fact remained: in two weeks, he stood to lose her.

* * *

Kent eased the Corvette into an empty slot in the parking lot at the restaurant. He walked around and opened the door and extended his hand to help Beth out. "You've been pretty quiet all the way here," he said. "Is something wrong?"

"Just business problems."

He eased his arm around her waist and steered her toward the restaurant. "Anything I can help you with?"

"Nothing that's legal." Before she could explain further, a voice about as welcome as fingernails scraping across a chalkboard came out of the evening.

"Bethany, we meet again so soon."

She forced a smile. "Alex."

Alex walked over to Kent and put out his hand. "I don't believe we've met. Alex Kirkland. I'm a colleague of Beth's."

"Kent McReynolds." He glanced at Beth. She was glaring.

"Are you coming or going, Alex?" Beth asked, taking a deep breath and forcibly adjusting the tone of her voice.

"Meeting someone for dinner." Kirkland took a few steps toward the door and held it open with his right hand. "Maybe you two would like to join us?" He made sure that he caught Beth's eye. "It's Rose Clancey."

The smug twinkle in his eyes made Beth's eyes widen. She knew he wanted her to explode and blow the deal. That, however, was not going to happen. After a short pause during which she fought for control, she put on her sweetest voice and said, "Actually, before you came up, we had just decided that we didn't want to eat here tonight. Isn't that right, Kent?"

Kent brushed off his initial surprise and played along. "Yes. As a matter of fact, we were just talking about another place." He turned his body so Kirkland couldn't see his face and gave Beth a puzzled look. "Where was that place again?"

"In Somerville." She peered back at Alex around Kent. "You will excuse us, won't you?" Then, slipping her arm through Kent's, she gently pulled him back toward the car. Halfway down the walkway, she stopped and turned back. "Alex, I do have a suggestion. Don't have the catch of the day—it just wouldn't be right." Kirkland smiled benignly and disappeared through the glass doors.

Beth crooked her arm toward Kent, beckoning him with a toss of her head to slip his arm through hers this time. "This place has suddenly lost its appeal. Shall we go?"

"What was that all about—'catch of the day'?"

"On Fridays," she explained, "the catch of the day at Willow's is usually grilled maco steak. Shark." She screwed up her nose and shook her head. "It would be a bit cannibalistic for Alex to eat one of his own kind, don't you agree?"

Beth took charge after leaving the parking lot of the restaurant. First stop was a deli. She had to rap on the front window to get the owner's attention, since it was after business hours, but a desperate plea and a good story got her two turkey and Swiss sandwiches on rye with mayo, some pickles and a couple of sodas. Next, she directed Kent to the Silvermeade complex and down the dirt road. Behind the bulldozers, dump trucks and backhoes was a partially built park.

They walked to the gazebo and sat on one of the wooden benches. "At least Kirkland won't spoil this dinner," Beth said, unwrapping one of the sandwiches and spreading the feast down between them.

"Is he as shifty as he seems?"

"Worse. I think his family roots go back to the snake in the tree at the Garden of Eden," she said, taking a bite from one of the pickles.

"He bears watching, then." Kent scanned the area. "I'm impressed. All your idea?"

"Mostly, but I had plenty of help with the design. One of the best suggestions came from Annie, my secretary."

"The cute blond with the spiked hair."

Beth laughed. "Underneath that hairdo is one smart young lady. Annie is into plants. Her apartment looks like a greenhouse. She began talking about how the tag 'endangered species' isn't limited to animals—some plants are in danger of extinction, too."

"Let me guess. She talked you into importing a jungle."

"Close." Beth pointed to one of the paths. "Down there will be a rainforest, as natural as we can get it for this area."

"With animals?"

"No animals." She pointed in another direction. "That way will be a flower preserve. Silvermeade will import hundreds of flowers from all over the world that will bloom at different times. That way, people can come here and see the place dressed for every season." She pointed behind him. "That's where an English garden will be. My Aunt Gerry likes those."

"You like building things."

"It's not the building I like as much as the planning. It fascinates me to start with an idea and work it through to reality." She stood. "Take this park. It began as a big dirt hole between the office complex and the mall. We knew when we added the hotel it would form a big triangle; the problem became what to do with it."

"Seems to me you'll need a lot of parking."

Beth shook her head firmly. "No. The office complex has a parking garage, and the hotel has underground parking facilities. But there *was* something else we needed."

"And that was?"

"Monuments."

"Monuments?"

"Monuments. To nature and all the living things we had to sacrifice to make way for the concrete and steel." Her voice became buoyant. "You see, it would be a give and take. We take some trees at first, but we give some back in the end. Something dies, something begins again."

Kent saw joy and determination sparkle in her eyes. "Sounds great."

"It may only be wishful thinking. The unfortunate reality is that unless the economy picks up and we fill the mall and the complex, the parkland may not survive. We may have to cut way back to survive." She watched Kent's smile fade and his face cloud with uneasiness. She shouldn't have said that—it only reminded them that the Congresswoman was pivotal to both their plans, and only one of them could win. She took a breath and changed the subject.

"Sorry about dinner." She lifted a slice of bread and looked woefully at its contents. "This is not exactly gourmet."

"Everything here suits me just fine," Kent said.

Beth smiled. "I'm glad I didn't let Alex ruin our evening." But as she looked at Kent, she was surprised to see the happiness fade from his eyes. "Is something wrong?"

"What gave me away?"

"You get this intense look on your face when you're deep in thought." She reached up and touched his cheek, her fingertips near his eye. "And right about here, you get a tiny twitch. It's almost like a nervous tic. It's actually kind of cute."

"That's the second time you said I'm cute. Do you mean it?"

A teasing sound crept into Beth's voice. "Actually, no. Puppies are cute. Blue Eagles are, well . . ." she cocked her head to the heavens, ". . . hardly cute. They're more ostentatious."

"That description matches one I heard a few days ago."

"From who?"

"Congresswoman Clancey." He paused for just a fraction of a second. "I have to ask this."

Beth studied him with searching concern. "Ask away."

"Are you going to reject me and help her out?"

Not honestly knowing the answer to his question, Beth lowered her eyes. "I do need her onboard at Silvermeade."

Kent straightened and sighed. "And I need her on my side." He put his hands on her shoulders before she could turn away. "Congresswoman Clancey is digging through everything to find reasons why the budget should be cut. She refuses to see the good the team can do for American morale."

"I gathered that much."

"And we have enough complications standing between us. I don't want any more."

Beth shifted uneasily, unsure of how to react. "That's fair. But there's something you should know about me before you go jumping to conclusions about us."

"What's that?"

She rose and walked over to the far side of the gazebo. "Do you see this?" She swept her hand in a large circle through the air. "This is my life. This concrete, steel, glass, wood and grass. These are tangible things." She faced him and leaned back onto the railing near one of the open sections. "Do you understand what I'm trying to say?"

"Frankly, no."

"What's between us is not tangible." She knew she was lying, if not to him, to herself. "We agreed on friendship, and somehow we let things get out of hand."

"Love is merely friendship that burst into flame." Kent strode over to her. "You don't seem to be the type of woman to go out with a man one night and turn her back on him the next."

"I'm not." She paused. "Wasn't." She fought the emotions that were threatening to break her voice and cause the tears that were filling her eyes to overflow. "You're only passing through my life, Kent. We both know that."

Kent reached up and brushed a teardrop away. "I've told you, I don't want to just pass through your life. I want to be a part of your life, and I want you to be part of mine." He took her chin between his thumb and forefinger and looked down into the blue skies of her eyes. "But I think that you're afraid to build something with me."

"Don't say that."

"Why? Because it's true?" He pulled her close, daring her to deny it.

Against her will, her hand reached up to caress his cheek. "I haven't thought about a relationship in a long time." More lies—she had dreamed about Kent almost constantly lately. "My life is here. I'm settled in, and I don't plan on going anywhere."

"What if I could stay here with you?" His voice was hushed, his eyes as innocent as a child's.

Beth put her fingers to his lips to silence him.

"Don't even say that. I won't be the one to lop off those mighty wings of yours. You'd be like a clipped bird, floundering in a cage, always looking to escape into the sky. Besides, it's too soon for either one of us to bargain and trade off dreams. How can we possibly know what we want yet?"

"I know I want you." Kent kissed the tips of her fingers as he spoke the words. "And I know you want me. But I'm willing to wait until you know it, too."

"It may be a very long wait."

"What if I quit flying?" Kent did not know how he found the courage to say the words.

"You couldn't stop flying—you tried it once and couldn't." Her heart slammed into her ribs. "We agreed on friendship. We should just enjoy it while it's ours to hold onto, accept what time we have and not grieve when it's over."

"I can still try to change your mind, can't I?"

"I can't promise that I'm capable of giving you anything more than right now."

He didn't argue with her. He just hugged her close. If she had looked into his eyes, she would have seen anger.

Anger in the way life chooses to test and tease.

Anger with the fact that he was in love with one stubborn lady.

And anger in the fact that he only had about two weeks left to get her to realize just how wrong she was.

Chapter Eleven

Kent leaned down to kiss her, but Beth stopped him. "We can't keep doing this."

"I'm only doing what all good pilots do."

"And that is?"

"Communicating my intentions."

"Communicating, huh?"

"There are many ways to talk without using the spoken word."

"And I'm sure you know each and every one of them." She gave him a discriminating glint. "After all, it *is* part of your job as a Blue Eagle to communicate well, no matter what the subject."

"I'm not doing a PR number on you," he said.

"I know you're not," she said softly. "But I make it a point of not falling into relationships headfirst anymore." She felt more like she was trying to convince herself. Teetering on the brink, she knew that with one tiny push she'd fall so hard that she'd never recover.

And would never want to. "I don't want either of us to get hurt."

"Getting hurt is part of life. You need the right person to come along to soothe the pain until it disappears forever."

"And you think you're the right person for me."

"No—I *know* that I am." His voice sounded firm, final.

Beth was shocked to see Kent's eyes suddenly fill with fierce sparkling. She clung to her decision, hoping her own eyes would not betray the fact that she knew he was probably right. "There's no use talking about this anymore," she said.

Kent heard the strained tone in Beth's voice and conceded that he may have lost this round in the battle. But as long as the war still raged, he felt he still had hope.

"I guess this is another stand-off," he conceded.

"I think you're right." Beth bit down on her lip. Tension stretched between them like a tight wire.

"Do you want me to take you home?" Kent asked slowly.

Her eyes were ice blue pools. "No."

"How about some coffee, then. On neutral ground in town."

She nodded. At least they'd have more time together.

After gathering the remnants of their dinner, they began the walk back to the car. Along the way, an all-out emotional war broke out inside Beth's head. The battle raged on and escalated in intensity, and by the time Kent had the car moving along the highway, Beth had a full blown headache. She thumped the heel of her hand on her forehead and groaned.

"What's that all about?" Kent asked.

Beth rolled her eyes and sighed in frustration.

"Headache from a poor attempt at getting two sides together in the cooperative spirit of Versailles."

"Want to talk about it?"

She pointed straight ahead and shook her head. "No more communicating for now. Just drive."

They settled on the coffee shop across from the Holiday Inn where Kent was staying. A slow love song, probably selected by the couple who had occupied the booth before them, played on the jukebox as Beth slowly sipped her coffee.

"Feel better?" Kent reached across and caressed her hand.

The gesture was sweet, making Beth smile. "Uh-huh, thanks."

"Want to tell me what's going on inside that head of yours?"

"A war."

"How big?"

Beth breathed an exasperated sigh, "Oh, let's see. It involves you, me, the United States government, and a snake in the grass named Kirkland." She put her fingertips to her temples and rubbed. "Not large enough to end democracy as we know it, but big enough to blow my life apart."

"Could get messy."

"I've been trying to tell you that."

"I think I can help you." Beth gave him a quizzical glance and he explained. "I have a copy of the reports I sent to the Congresswoman. You can look them over when you have time."

She shook her head, subconsciously aware of the dull ache that the memories of the papers produced. "I've already read them, Kent."

"Then read them again. There might be something you missed, something that could help you cement your business with Clancey."

Beth rested an elbow on the table and propped her chin on her knuckles. She studied Kent's face unhurriedly, feature by feature. "Why would you share secrets with me? We could end up on opposite sides of this issue."

Kent looked into Beth's eyes and saw something deeply serious there. "I know," he said. "But I think you need to have those papers even if you choose not to use them." He stood and extended his hand to her. "Want to come with me to get them?"

The protective shield came up quickly in Beth's eyes. "I think I'll wait here."

"Okay. I'll just be a minute."

Beth watched Kent leave the coffee shop, his handsome features and striking appearance turning the heads of a few young women coming inside. As he held the door open for them, Beth could not help but notice the admiration in their eyes. She wasn't trying to eavesdrop as they passed her table, but their brazen assessment of Kent came through loud and clear.

Their vocal appraisal struck a nerve. She knew the pleasure a person could derive from appreciating Kent's physical qualities, but she was also well aware of the inner beauty of that same man; the beautiful qualities that made up his spirit.

I must be insane! Beth thought, slamming her hand onto the table. *I'm wasting the precious time we have left.* She signaled for the waitress.

"Can I get you something, sugar?" the brassy-haired woman asked, pulling out her order pad. She pointed her pencil at the empty seat. "Did Handsome stick you with the check?"

"Actually, no," she said, handing her a five dollar bill. It was Beth's turn to spin a few heads as she raced out of the coffee shop. She sped across the parking lot into the lobby of the Holiday Inn, running right into Kent as he was coming back.

"Couldn't wait to see me, huh?" he quipped.

"For a pilot, you have a very romantic imagination, Captain."

"And for a professional planner, you seem to do a lot of things on impulse, Miss Clarke. But I have to admit, before I left the coffee shop, I thought about throwing you over my shoulder and carrying you off."

"Cave-man tactics?"

"No," he said with a twinkle in his eye, "search and rescue."

"Rescue?" She arched an eyebrow. "From what?"

"From all those stupid consequences we seem to keep alluding to each time we're together."

She shook her head. "Captain McReynolds, I believe that the Air Force is right—you could sell anything to anybody."

"The only thing I want to sell you right now is us." He whispered the words into her ear and kissed them into place.

"I'm afraid."

Beth felt the sigh of his breath on her cheek as he spoke. "There's nothing to be afraid of."

But fear still held an iron grip on her heart. To her, this fairy tale romance just seemed too fragile for the real world. "I'm afraid of failing again, of finding out again that happily-ever-after only happens in books."

"You could never fail me, honey."

Beth's eyes searched Kent's face. "Are you sure this thing between us is real?" A feeling of hope flowed from her voice into her heart, carving his name there for all time.

"I want to show you just how real it is, if you'll let me," he said.

Chapter Twelve

As Beth pressed the button for the elevator in the lobby of the Silvermeade Complex, she still stubbornly refused to believe that she had lost control. After all, a relationship could be planned just like anything else, couldn't it?

As the elevator doors opened on her floor, Annie was passing by with a tray of coffee and danish.

"Company?" Beth asked, running to keep up with her.

"Yep. Clancey."

"I knew she was going to check on the final preparations for the reception, but I thought that wasn't going to happen until Friday," Beth pushed open the door to her office and allowed Annie to enter first.

"One of her staffers called about five minutes ago and moved up the meeting." Annie slid the tray onto the credenza in Beth's office. "I knew you would tell her to come down, so I did."

"Good job, Annie. We're close to getting her signature on the lease, so whatever the Congresswoman wants . . ."

". . . the Congresswoman gets." Annie held up her hand and Beth slapped a high-five, their ritual symbol of a job-well-done. "Oh, before I forget, Clancey's staffer also asked to use one of the conference rooms for some high-powered meeting after the reception, and asked that you be there. I told her okay on both."

Beth dropped into her desk chair. "I was afraid of this."

Annie quickly slid into a seat opposite her. "What?"

Beth blew out a long breath of air. "I have a feeling the Congresswoman may call in her marker at that meeting. She hinted about helping her shoot down the Blue Eagles."

"But aren't you helping the pilot save them?"

"Yes." Beth's fingers drummed the desktop nervously. "I've been making calls for the past few days. He's been great about keeping me in the background."

"Did you ask him to do that?"

"No," Beth smiled, despite what she was feeling. "He wants to make it as easy on me as he can."

Annie inclined her head. "And I thought chivalry was dead."

"Not with Kent, it isn't."

"Apparently. But now what?"

"I'm not sure," Beth said, getting up from the chair. She rubbed her hands on her arms and paced as she spoke.

Annie shook her head. "While you're at it, better watch your back too. Kirkland's had been hanging around the Congresswoman like a fly on sugar. He's up to something."

Beth rubbed her fingernails with her thumb nervously. "I don't think the Congresswoman would pull a switch on me at this late date. She has a good reputation for keeping her word."

Annie forced a tight smile of her own.

"I don't want to worry you, but I heard Kirkland has an appointment with the top boss."

Beth's brow furrowed instantly. "Any ideas on it?"

"Nope, but scuttlebutt has it that Kirkland's in hot water."

Beth moved back to her desk, her jaw tightening. "That means he's going to try even harder to steal someone's thunder. I'll feel better when the ink is dry on the lease with Clancey."

Annie crossed her fingers. "Good luck." She rose and leaned her hands onto the desk. "How are things with the pilot?"

Beth's smile answered the question before her words did. "Everything considered, great."

"Looks to me like you're falling without a net."

"It's not like that at all."

"Oh no? I think you're in love, Boss."

With her heart hammering at the idea that it was so obvious, Beth did her best to brush the idea aside. "We have an understanding. We'll enjoy each other for the time he's here, and then shake hands and say goodbye when it's time for him to leave. An arrangement like that doesn't translate into love."

Annie walked around to Beth's side of the desk, and with arms folded across her chest, looked Beth square in the eye. "Are you sure that's what *he* feels?"

Beth tossed her head and gave a restless tug on her sleeve. "He likes me," she reluctantly admitted.

Annie snorted, very unladylike, but very effective in getting her point across. "Right."

"Okay, he likes me a lot." Beth rose and moved to the window, looking out so Annie couldn't read her eyes.

"And he agreed to your screwed-up terms?"

Beth sighed, long and hard, sending a lock of hair just above her eyes in motion. "He knows how I feel."

"And you expect him to just walk away."

"I do." True, Kent made her happy, made her feel safe and—dare she admit it—loved. But, love normally works two ways. Could she make him feel happy and loved if every waking moment was filled with thoughts of danger and death while he was flying? How could she possibly handle his going on missions? Could Kent stand such a strained committment and still give the concentration he needed to the sky? She closed her eyes to discourage the tears she felt forming, and answered her own question. *No. It wouldn't be possible.* "It's because," she finally continued, turning back to Annie, "I know what's best for both of us over the long haul."

"Well, I think you're crazy." Annie walked toward the door. "If I had someone like that interested in me, I'd never let him leave my sight."

Walking down the hall toward Beth's office, Kent was beginning to feel edgy. Normally he wasn't a man who kept an eye on time, but time was ticking away. He only had a few days left. Soon, it would be down to mere hours. The practice session at McGuire Air Force Base was scheduled for Friday, the show the next day. He had hoped by now that he and Beth would have settled their relationship. So why hadn't they?

He had done exactly as she had asked. Didn't press her, gave her the space she needed, and tried to give her the attention and emotional support as a foundation they could build upon. He kept her part in his mission to a bare minimum and encouraged her to follow her business instincts when dealing with Congresswoman Clancey.

But her heart's instincts were the problem. Getting her to commit was turning into a bigger job than saving the Blue Eagles, and unfortunately he didn't have much time left for calculated maneuvers. A slow, steady approach laced with love and understanding was a luxury he just couldn't afford much longer. For him, it was beginning to look more like full-speed-ahead time.

He put his hand on the wall just outside her door and took a deep breath. One way or another, he was going to get this relationship off the ground and in the air where it belonged. Giving himself the thumbs-up just for luck, he stepped inside the reception area of Beth's office, ready to do just that.

"Well, hello handsome," Annie said when she saw him, rolling out the words as she pushed back from her desk and hooked an arm over the back of her chair. "I suppose it's too much to hope that you're here to see me."

Kent leaned against the door and grinned. "Is Beth in?"

Annie pointed to the closed office door. "She's in a conference." She dipped forward, eased her elbows onto her desk and placed her chin in her hands. "You can stay here with me and wait if you'd like."

Kent turned up his smile and nodded. "I'd like."

"Good. Coffee?"

"No thanks."

"I suppose that little box in your hand isn't for me."

Kent settled into the deep leather cushions of one of the chairs near Annie's desk. "Sorry."

A twinkle came into Annie's eyes. "What is it?"

A larger twinkle set into Kent's. "It's a surprise."

"You aren't going to tell me what's in there, are you?"

Kent chuckled and slipped the box into his jacket pocket. " 'Fraid not. It's for Beth."

"Where have you been all my life?" Annie asked.

Kent pointed straight up with his forefinger. "Around."

Annie snapped her fingers. "You're him."

"Him?"

"*Her* him," Annie said, playfully pointing to Beth's office door.

Sunshine broke across Kent's face as he flashed her another one of his dazzling smiles. "You found me out."

"Uh-huh. Beth said you were great-looking, but she neglected to say just *how* great-looking."

The sound of the inner office door opening turned both their heads. Head down, with fingers flipping through a file folder, Beth emerged. "Annie, could you call security for me? My aunt's cutting through the park again. With all the new digging out there, I'm afraid she may trip or fall into a hole."

"You have a visitor," Annie said sweetly.

"Hi," Kent said as Beth lifted her head from the papers.

"He's got something for you," Annie said. "Open it. I gotta see what it is."

With a toss of her head Beth motioned to the door. "Security, Annie."

Annie straightened to military attention and saluted. "Right away." She turned to Kent and put on her sweetest smile. "Do come back, any time." Before Beth could say another word, she bolted for the door and left the room.

"She's something," Kent said, taking a step closer to Beth.

She felt the soft brush of Kent's fingertips against her cheek. She slid the file folder she was holding onto Annie's desk and traced the line of Kent's jaw with her fingers as he gathered her into his arms. "Is this another one of your spontaneous displays of affection?"

"Hardly. I've been planning it all morning."

Beth flicked her head toward her office. "Suppose Madame Congresswoman came out here and saw us like this?"

"Then she'd *really* have something to report back to the Senate, wouldn't she?" He drew away from her and winked.

Beth laughed. "Did you come here to distract me?"

Putting a hand into his pocket, Kent took out the box and handed it to her. "No. I wanted you to have this."

Beth suddenly felt shy as she ran her hand over the grey velvet lid. "You bought something for me? How sweet."

"It was a gift to me from an Indian friend back in Arizona. I want you to have it."

Beth expected an arrowhead necklace or something similar when she opened the box, but what she found instead was a pale white amulet in the shape of a bird, hanging from a golden chain. "It's beautiful."

Kent took it from her and fastened it around her neck as he spoke. "It's carved from the bone of an eagle. An old chief named Thundercloud gave it to me. Indian legend says that the spirit of the bird will protect you from danger."

Beth's voice dropped to a whisper. "Maybe you should keep it, then." She reached up to remove the chain from her neck, but Kent stopped her with a touch of his hand.

"No. It looks great on you."

Beth fingered the amulet. "I don't know what to say."

"Thank you is enough."

As Kent's fingertips touched the charm at her throat, Beth thought she'd never be able to breathe again. She willed herself to draw in some air and whispered, "Thanks."

"Are we still on for later?" Kent asked, content just to look at the happiness in her eyes.

"I hope so. I still have a few more details to iron out with her, and then I have a meeting at four."

"And I have a PR tour to do. Can we meet at six?"

"Make it seven,"

"Seven, then," he said. "I'll pick you up." Their eyes met and caught, and a wide smile crossed Kent's face.

"What?" she asked, puzzled.

"You're mine, you know. So you'd better get used to the idea." Then, before she could protest, he was gone.

She leaned back onto the wall while she pondered not only his confidence but also his constant appeal. Her heart took a sudden perilous leap and it made her wonder. *What was this thing called love really all about? Was it making sacrifices and doing what was best for the other, no matter how you felt? Or was it defying the odds just to be together?*

She fingered the carved bird resting near her heart and thought about its meaning. She'd wear his gift for now, but tonight she would give it back to him. With his career, he needed the power of its protection more than she did.

"Thank you for the use of your phone," Congress-woman Clancy said, emerging from Beth's office.

Her voice barely penetrated Beth's mind. She had

been concentrating on Kent. She spun around and gathered her composure. "Not a problem."

"I have an appointment in about thirty minutes, and just enough time to make it if I leave right now," the Congresswoman said. "Perhaps we can wrap this up on Friday. You *are* coming to my meeting, aren't you?"

"I have it in my book," Beth said.

"A few of my supporters are flying in from Washington, and I'm counting on you to help me answer any questions they might have about the accident at Indian Springs."

"The official report has all the answers you need."

"All the *official* answers maybe, but none with a personal slant on the tragedy. I need your input on that."

Beth could not rally quick enough to protest. "I'll be at your meeting," she repeated.

"Good." Rose-Clancey extended her hand. "I'm sure we can conclude our business after that. Until the reception, good day Miss Clarke."

Beth snapped her mouth shut, stunned and angered by the Congresswoman's implication. As she watched the Congresswoman leave, her mind spun back to the report that Kent had given her almost a week earlier. She hadn't been able to open it, but tonight she would read it from cover to cover until she knew every word forward and backward. Lease or no lease, she was not going to let anyone back her into a corner.

She was so angry about falling into Rose Clancey's trap that she never heard the commotion in the hallway until one of the sales managers ran into her as she came out of her office. He was out of breath and a little pale.

"Miss Clarke, it's your aunt. She fell."

"Where?"

"In the park."

"Is she all right? What happened?" Beth's heart rose up and blocked off her breath. She ran to the elevator with the sales manager right behind her.

"Security has called for an ambulance."

"How bad is it?"

"I don't know for sure. Someone said she hit her head. They're taking her to the medical center. Annie went with her."

Beth grabbed his arm. "Listen. Call the secretarial pool and get someone to cover my office and cancel my four o'clock. I'm going to the hospital. Have someone call my uncle. His work number is on my Rolodex under Carter, Joseph Carter."

"I'll take care of it," the young man called out.

Through the clear back panel on the outside elevator Beth could see the ambulance pulling away from the dirt road in the park. She closed her eyes and whispered a silent prayer. Since Indian Springs, everyone and everything was acutely important to her; her appreciation of life sharper, more meaningful. She couldn't bear the thought of losing someone again.

Especially not her Aunt Gerry.

Chapter Thirteen

When Beth arrived at the hospital, the Emergency Room doctor told her that her aunt was in X-ray and was being admitted as a precautionary measure. She went straight to Gerry's room. "I need to make sure she has everything she needs," she said, rummaging through her handbag for her checkbook.

"What I need is a nice hot cup of tea," Gerry said from behind her.

Beth turned, and a huge smile relaxed the tension that lined her face. "Aunt Gerry, you're . . ." her eyes settled on the snowy white cast on her aunt's left arm, ". . . not going to be able to crochet for a while, are you?"

"No," Gerry said, as the hospital escort helped her out of the wheelchair and into the bed.

Beth pulled a well-worn chair closer to the bed and gave her aunt a peck on her cheek before sitting down.

"I was worried to death about you. No one would tell me much of anything."

"I'll be just fine," Gerry said, squirming to a sitting position. "Honey, raise the head of the bed for me, please." She cocked her thumb to the wall behind her. "I think the controls are hanging somewhere up there."

"I told you something like this might happen if you didn't use the connecting tube," she scolded over the whine of the electric motor underneath the bed.

"I told you I don't like that thing."

Beth fastened the control unit to her aunt's pillow by its metal clip. "If you used it, you wouldn't be here now, would you?" Gerry waved off her words with a swipe of her good hand. Satisfied her point was made, Beth continued. "Where's Annie?"

Gerry poked the pillow to a more comfortable shape with her free hand. "I sent her to the coffee shop." She frowned. "I do hope the tea tastes better than the coffee."

Beth grinned. "Ornery to the end." She folded her arms across her chest. "Now that I know you'll be all right, I want to know what on earth you were thinking? You know construction's been stepped up."

"You know how I hate that glass thing they put up."

"That 'glass thing' was put there for safety."

"Let me rephrase it then. You know how I like being outside." she paused and waited for a response from her niece. The only one that came was a narrowing of Beth's eyes. "Well, I was coming to see you, and out of the corner of my eye I saw this guy on an earthmover. And for a minute I thought it was Kent."

Beth's mouth fell open. "Why on earth would Kent be on a bulldozer in my parkland?"

Gerry threw up her free hand. "Now that's just what *I* was wondering." Her features became animated. "I had to be sure. You know me."

"I sure do."

"Do you want to hear this or not?"

Beth settled herself down in a chair. "Wild horses couldn't drag me away before you finish."

Gerry's hand gestured in a sweeping motion. "Anyway, so there I was, walking toward that young man, squinting to get a real good look, and *kee-rash!* The next thing I know I'm rolling down a big hole. How it got in front of me, I just don't know. It wasn't there before."

Beth shook her head in dismay. "You're lucky you didn't do more than just break your arm."

"I did." Gerry looked at her sheepishly. She pointed to an area behind her left ear. "Six stitches."

Beth's eyes grew large, her voice pitched a little higher. "You could have been killed!" The truth in the words suddenly settled around her stomach and with a hard squeeze. Much like the result of an iron grip on a wet sponge, she felt instantly drained.

"You don't look too good yourself, dear," Gerry said in response to the loss of color in Beth's face.

Fearful images of what could have happened built quickly in Beth's mind. "I'm going to alert security. If you ever go tramping around in the park again before it's done, I'm going to have you physically carried off the grounds. Do you understand?"

Gerry nodded. "Okay, you win." Her voice became suddenly serious. "If I promise, I need you to promise something for me."

Worried again, Beth rose and sat on the edge of her aunt's bed. "Anything. You know that."

Gerry turned her head and pointed to the large, shaved spot at the site of the stitches. "You have to help me cover these."

"Hey, look on the bright side," a voice behind them said, "I could shave a few more little circles all over your head, Mrs. Carter, and create a whole new look."

Even though she was upset, Beth laughed as she pictured her aunt in her new hairdo. "You're not thinking of trading in *your* spikes for some polka dots, are you Annie?"

Annie placed an insulated cup full of hot tea on the bedside table. "Why not, it could catch on."

"I could use a new hairdo," Gerry said. "Maybe I'll cover this gray and become a redhead."

As both women burst into laughter, Beth just shook her head, partly in admiration, partly in surrender. Gerry saw a silver lining in everything. If only she could be more like that. The silver linings in her life were few and far in between.

"Do you need anything for the night, Aunt Gerry?" Beth asked. "A robe, some slippers?"

"No thanks, dear." She smoothed the crisp, white cotton gown given to her in the emergency room. "This will be just fine."

"I can run to the farmhouse and get some of your things."

"Don't bother. I'm only staying overnight, and I'm not planning on being here long enough to need anything else." Gerry's eyes suddenly lit from inside. "Oh, I almost forgot—I think I saw Kent in the emergency room while I was waiting outside X-ray for an escort."

"Like you saw him on the earthmover?" Beth asked.

"No. I really saw him this time. He's in the hospital."

Almost in tandem with her aunt's words, blood began to slide through Beth's veins like cold needles. Her heart rose to her throat, and her whole body seemed to tighten with the fleeting thought that somehow, something had happened to Kent, too.

"Hey, you okay?" Annie asked, noticing the change on Beth's face. "Maybe *you* should be in the bed instead of your aunt."

"Is he hurt?.," she managed to say over the thudding of her heart. Her mind spun in a hundred directions at once and she couldn't decide if the sirens in her head were real or just a figment of memory. Was Kent here for emergency treatment? Had he been flying? Did he crash?

"I don't think so," Gerry said, apparently not noticing the panic her words had caused Beth. "He was here with that Congress lady. They were just vanishing around the corner with a bunch of hospital bigwigs when I was wheeled into the hall. I don't think he saw me. The Congresswoman waved, but didn't stop."

As if a tight band around her chest snapped, Beth's heart fell back into place. She took a long, slow breath of relief. *See, it had been silly to assume Kent had been hurt. He and the Congresswoman were likely doing some PR work, that's all.*

"The Congresswoman probably knows that you're a Republican," Beth said lightly as her ghosts vanished again.

Gerry laughed. "Guess so. She probably didn't want to waste her time on someone who voted for the other guy. You saw them, didn't you Annie?"

" 'Fraid not, Mrs. C.," Annie said shaking her head. "I must have been concentrating on your tea order."

"Well, it *was* Kent," Gerry insisted. "I'd recognize him anywhere after all the time he has spent with us lately." Then she yawned. "Excuse me. I guess the medication they gave me is starting to hit. I'm more tired than I thought."

"Feel better, honey," Annie said, turning to leave. "See you at the office, Beth."

Beth nodded as Annie disappeared into the hallway. She turned back to Gerry. "Uncle Joe will be here soon. I'm going to let you get some rest." Tucking the blankets around her Aunt's shoulders, Beth kissed her forehead. "Are you sure there isn't anything you need?"

Aunt Gerry pulled her mouth into a smile. "Well, you could get me a romance novel from the gift shop. There isn't much to do here at the hospital, and if I can't crochet, at least I can read. Maybe even pick up a few romance tips."

Beth was barely able to keep the laughter from her face as she tried to appear serious. "Aunt Gerry, you're terrible."

Gerry winked. "Joe doesn't think so. That's why we've been married forty years so far."

On the way down to the gift shop, Beth thought of how panicked she had become just thinking that Kent might be hurt. It was an instinctive emotional reaction, one that still left her shaken. As involuntary as it was, it proved one thing: if she responded this intensely at just the *thought* of Kent being hurt, she was nowhere near ready to handle the situation if it actually happened.

Before today, she only feared that she could never be the kind of woman Kent needed in his life—now she knew for sure.

Kent McReynolds, Number Two, Left Wing, dressed in his snappy dark blue flight suit, walked into the last hospital room on the fourth floor. Tom Lowry, acting as escort and carrying the Blue Eagle pamphlets, moved directly to the patients and handed each a copy.

"I could get used to this," Lowry whispered as he passed Kent on his way to the other side of the ward. "Where do I sign up?"

Kent finished talking to an older man with his leg in traction before answering. "See your Air Force recruiter, son."

"Right." The NCO rolled his eyes and walked over to Congresswoman Clancey as Kent moved on to the next bed.

Rose Clancey was listening intently to the patient in bed three tell Kent how wonderful it must feel to dedicate one's life to making other people proud. She almost cracked a smile as the patient quickly added that the Blue Eagles seem to be one of the only good things about paying all those tax dollars to the government.

"It's nice, isn't it," Lowry said, turning to Rose and seizing the opportunity to underline what the patient just said. "The people here are getting to see a real live hero."

Rose Clancey was not a woman to give in too quickly. "I suppose it has its merits."

"Just look at that man's wife. She's practically swooning. Betcha the next time she votes, it won't be for someone who supports a big budget cut that cuts the Eagles out." Lowry grimaced as the Congresswoman shot a rapier glance in his direction. "Sorry, what I meant was, that she's going to be telling everyone for weeks to come that she met a real live Blue Eagle pilot. You know, ma'am, folks say the Eagles represent what's good about America. Maybe even what's good about democracy."

"Perhaps," the Congresswoman said without much animation. It was all that she cared to acknowledge aloud. Lowry was more correct than she cared to admit.

"Hey, Tom," Kent called out from across the room, "I need a few more pamphlets to autograph for some of John's friends in Rocky Hill. Do we have any extras?"

"Right here," the NCO said.

As he watched Lowry walk toward him, Kent tried

to contain his smile. This was the part he really liked best; relating to the people, meeting them, talking to them, watching them beam with pride just thinking about their country. It was the same pride he carried in his heart just by wearing the uniform and flying for America. He loved it—loved it all.

He also got a kick out of what was going to happen next, as he took the pamphlets from Lowry's hand and said, "By the way, Sarge, John here wants your autograph, too."

"Mine?" The NCO's eyes lit up and his face brightened. "No one's ever asked for my autograph before."

"Get used to it. Even Blue Eagle NCO's are part of the famous family."

Lowry's chest seemed to puff up all of its own accord. "Why sure, John." He turned to the bed-ridden patient. "I'd be happy to sign a flyer for you."

Kent glanced at the Congresswoman out of the corner of his eye and grinned broadly. He was winning this cold war; she was finally thawing. He could see it all over her face.

Outside the hospital, the photographer from the local newspaper raised his camera. "Just one more picture. Congresswoman, a smile this time?"

Kent stood still and smiled at the lens for about the hundredth time. He was in a hurry to get back to his room and out of his flight suit. He hoped this picture was the last.

"Can I drop you somewhere, Madame Congresswoman?" he asked, after their PR tour of the hospital was over.

"No, Captain, but there is something you can do for me. I saw Miss Clarke's secretary talking to an elderly woman in a wheelchair outside of the X-ray department earlier. Maybe it was her mother. I've been dealing quite a bit with Ms. Potts lately, and I've become quite fond of her. I even tried to take her away from Ms. Clarke, but she refused." The Congresswoman nodded in approval. "I like loyalty. The girl has a fine head on her shoulders. Ms. Clarke is lucky to have her."

Kent agreed. "Annie's a special lady. Beth considers her an important part of the team. But if I remember correctly, Ms. Potts' mother lives out west."

"Perhaps another relative, then. Maybe an aunt."

Not knowing why, Kent glanced up at the five-story hospital, a chill running up his spine. "An older woman, you say?"

"Yes."

A fleeting thought danced across Kent's mind. "Gray hair, bright eyes, great smile?" Kent asked anxiously.

"Sounds about right."

"She wasn't hurt, was she?"

"She looked fine except for a cast on her arm. She may have even gone home by now. Do you mind checking?"

"Not at all."

Kent turned to leave but was halted by the sound of the Congresswoman's voice. "Oh, and Captain, don't forget the reception on Thursday. If you look as handsome in full dress uniform as you do in that flight suit, you just might be able to talk me into siding with you."

Kent turned back and saluted her. "If that's a promise, I'll be there, ma'am." The reception, though not something he would have chosen to do under other circumstances, would give him a chance to make a few pitches of his own to her colleagues. "You can count on it."

Rose Clancey smiled. "I'll call you with the details later."

She extended her hand. "A very informative tour, Captain."

"Thank you."

As he watched the Congresswoman leave, another crack appeared in his plan. If he was going to the reception in full dress uniform, he had to be sure to tell Beth about it tonight. He had been so careful not to wear his uniform around her, as a consequence of their reunion. He wanted Beth to love or reject the man before she remembered that the uniform came along with him.

As Beth stepped off the elevator on the third floor, she saw a small crowd of nurses gathered outside her aunt's room. When she got closer, it was apparent the nurses were delighted, not concerned.

"What's going on?" she asked when she got near the door.

"Mrs. Carter has a visitor. A good-looking one, I might add. But he only has eyes for her—we can't even get his attention," one of the nurses said, stepping back to let Beth peek inside. On tip-toes Beth leaned forward, but when she got a clear view inside, the whole world suddenly stopped moving.

Kent was near the foot of the hospital bed, hands behind his back, standing at ease, still in his flight suit. He was talking to Gerry, eyes focused on her face, apparently drawing on his military training to not allow himself to be distracted by the clamor in the hall.

As Beth's eyes welded to his handsome profile, he smiled as he acknowledged something her aunt said, and suddenly it wasn't Kent anymore—it was David. Like a slow frame-by-frame advancement of movie film, the two faces interchanged in Beth's mind, freezing her to the spot and numbing her feelings.

All her illusions were abruptly torn asunder and a scream clawed in her throat, fighting for the freedom that would never be given. David had come back to life in a nightmare she couldn't stop. He was here with her, flesh and blood, holding her hostage with images of the past, and reminding her that the pain and terror could become a real part of her future.

As her head began to spin with memories, she somehow regained control and took a few shaky steps outside so Kent would not see her. Leaning onto the wall for support, she felt the tears she had held back for so long break free. A tortured sob escaped her lips as she slowly put more distance between herself and Gerry's room; between herself and the driving pain.

"Are you okay?" A passing nurse reached out and grabbed onto Beth to support her.

Beth swallowed a sob and turned away so the nurse wouldn't see the tears. "I just need some air. I'll be fine." Squaring her shoulders, she pushed the clouded memories aside. "Please, give this to Mrs. Carter in 316," she said, thrusting the paperback novel toward the nurse and holding herself rigid, her jaw tight to contain her turmoil. "She's my aunt."

A curious look crossed the nurse's face as she took it. "Are you sure you don't want to give it to her yourself?"

"No. I have to go," Beth explained as she turned to leave. Then suddenly she spun back. "Give this to her too," she said, unfastening the gold chain that held Kent's amulet against her throat. "And please tell my aunt I'll call her later." Looking even more confused, the nurse nodded.

Beth's glance jerked in the direction of her aunt's room as she watched the nurse walk down the hall.

She couldn't face Kent now, maybe not ever again. The pain that squeezed her heart at the sight of him in uniform was nearly unbearable. Her hands shook as she frantically pressed the elevator call button. She had been a fool to think she could ignore what was real. Seeing Kent in his Blue Eagle flight suit had only amplified what she had been trying so hard to mute.

There could never be anything for them together. Not while he still belonged to the sky.

Chapter Fourteen

"Do you always create this much of a stir?" Gerry asked Kent as two more volunteers in candy-striped coats elbowed their way to the front for a better look.

The corners of Kent's mouth dimpled with a smile. "It's the uniform. Take off this flight suit and I'm just an ordinary guy."

Gerry's glance wandered back to the hospital door. "That's not what they think." Gerry crooked a forefinger to call him closer to her bed. She lowered her voice to a whisper. "Some of those ladies are looking at you like you're Tom Cruise in *Top Gun*."

Kent's laughter was full-hearted. "There's just one lady I wish would look at me like that."

"She's here somewhere, you know."

Kent's right hand flew to his chest as though it could hide what he was wearing. "She is?"

"Yes. Something wrong?"

"I hope not." Kent suddenly felt very conspicuous

in his attire. He took a quick look over his shoulder and was relieved that none of the faces at the door belonged to Beth. "I just don't want her to see me in uniform yet."

"Considering how long it's taken her to find a suitable man, uniform or not, there's no sense putting off what has to happen."

"I haven't been putting things off . . ." his voice trailed off. Maybe he had been. Fear of losing something precious has a way of doing that to a man. "Do you know where she is?" he asked in a low voice, his eyes moving automatically toward the doorway.

"I sent her out to get me something to read."

Kent nodded, his thoughts far off. He had planned to ease Beth's re-entry into the military world by talking to her about the Air Force at dinner tonight. Then, if all went well, he would wear his uniform in front of her. Her transition back had to be slow and gentle. There was still time to salvage that plan, but only if he got out of the hospital before she saw him.

He instinctively straightened to attention, now that he was military again. "I'd better get going."

Gerry held a hand up to stop him from leaving. "I don't think it's going to be easy for you to get out of here in one piece, with all your admirers at the door. You'll need a little help from me." She crooked her finger again and brought him closer. "Thank you, dear," she said loudly, kissing him on the cheek, "give that kiss to my daughter and the children." Her voice rose just a bit more. "Those six grandchildren you two have given me really keep me young."

The groan from the nurses jamming the doorway could have drowned out the hospital pager. Slowly they began to disperse.

"Thanks," Kent said saluting, "And I thought Norman Schwartzkopf cleared out the Gulf pretty fast."

He winked. "Could have taken days off the war if he had talked to you first."

Gerry blew on her nails and brushed them on her hospital gown. "I know." She shooed him out with a flick of her free hand. "Now go on, get out of here. I'm a pretty good reader of body language, and yours says antsy."

As Kent left the room, the nurse entering gave Kent an obvious once over. He smiled at her politely before hurrying down the hall. "Umm-umm! A man like that can give you a whole new definition of handsome," she said as she set a tray on Gerry's bed table.

"I suppose if I were younger I might agree with you."

The nurse smiled and pulled a romantic suspense novel out of her pocket. "This is from your niece. She got as far as the door and then suddenly decided to leave. I don't think she felt well."

Gerry took the book and set it on her bed tray. She tried to keep her voice composed. "Did she say anything?"

The nurse held out the white amulet, the totem appearing to suspend itself in the air on its own. "Only that she wanted you to have this, too. Quite frankly, I didn't think she was going to make it to the elevator. Is she ill?"

Gerry took the necklace and then fell back into her pillow, a worried expression crossing her face. "I'm afraid she might have something medical science can't cure."

"Rare disease?"

"Worse. Broken dreams."

There was a light coming from one of the second floor windows of the farmhouse, and Beth's car was in the driveway. Kent breathed a sigh of relief. When she didn't show up for dinner, he feared she'd been in an accident. With that possibility out of the way there was only one other explanation: she had been among the mass of nurses crowding Gerry's doorway. He could forget all the strategy he had been carefully formulating over the past few days.

On the way up to her apartment, his footsteps on the wooden stairs sounded like an explosion of mortar fire. When he finally got to the top floor landing, he froze, hand poised in the air, ready to knock on the door. A hundred thoughts flew through his mind, and he knew he could ponder them for eternity and still not know what to do until he faced her. So he knocked, not really expecting her to answer. After a few minutes, he knew that it would take nothing short of a miracle to get him inside.

And he knew only one person qualified to perform a honest-to-goodness miracle right now. Aunt Gerry.

When Kent entered Gerry's room she was just hanging up the telephone. "That was Beth," she said. I'm afraid she doesn't want to see you, Kent." Her voice was firm, but her face told Kent she hoped he wouldn't give up and go away.

"But I have to see her."

"Why?"

"I want to marry her, ma'am." It was a sudden admission that left even Kent reeling after the words were spoken.

Gerry, however, did not seem the least bit surprised. "I thought as much. Have you asked her yet?"

"No. I wanted to wait until I was sure that the uniform would not make a difference."

"Under other circumstances, I wouldn't argue with that." Gerry raised herself to a sitting position. "But as I said earlier, I think you may have been a little too cautious. Now the question is, what are we going to do about it?"

"Ma'am?" Hope spread across his face.

She motioned Kent to sit down on the bed. "It's my guess that Beth is panicking right now from being in love, and being afraid to be in love."

"Then I have to talk to her," he insisted, rising and taking one of Gerry's hands, "before I lose her completely."

"You want me to get you inside her apartment, don't you?"

Kent nodded. "Either that, or, and I am sorry ma'am, but I will have to forcibly open the door."

Gerry reached over, opened the nightstand and snatched her purse from the top drawer. "I thought you might say something like that." She rummaged through the well-worn tapestry handbag before finding the apartment door key and patting it into Kent's hand. "But before you go," she put her hand into a compartment in the purse, "I have to give you this." Holding up the carved amulet, her face darkened with emotion. "Beth thought you might be coming by to see me and asked that if you did, I return this to you. She said you need it more than she does."

Kent responded to the question in Gerry's eyes. "It's a talisman of protection given to me by an old Indian chief back in Arizona. I gave it to Beth, thinking it might help her accept what I do. Sometimes, holding something tightly in our hands when things get rough gives us the strength we need."

"It seems it couldn't give Beth the strength she needs to believe in her heart." Gerry dropped the necklace into Kent's palm. "But that doesn't mean she won't change her mind, now does it?" Curling his large fingers around the slender chain, Gerry smiled. "And I would like that. She needs you, even if she doesn't realize it yet. I would hate for her to realize it after you've gone from her life."

"Thank you." Kent leaned over and kissed Gerry on the cheek. "But I'm not going anywhere. At least, not without Beth."

Kent quietly closed the door to Beth's apartment behind him and stopped abruptly when her saw her. She was sitting on the sofa, clutching a throw pillow to her chest and looking out the window into the night sky. He stood immobile inside the archway. When she turned and their eyes met, he felt a split second of unfamiliar panic. With slow strides, he went to her. With each step he took closer, he searched her eyes for a sign of objection. Happily, he could find none.

"I was worried when you didn't meet me at the Willows." His voice was cool, careful to modify any emotion that might send the wrong message.

She wiped at the tears that were running down her cheeks. "I had to think."

"Are you okay?"

"Okay?" she asked stiffly. "No, I'm not okay."

Kent continued to study her. He could see her cheeks flush. "I'm sorry," he said, "I didn't mean . . . it hadn't occurred to me . . . I didn't want . . . if only . . . heck, help me out here." He raked his fingers though his tousled hair and then ran his hand across the back of his neck.

Beth sighed and tried to smile. "You aren't the one who should be sorry. You are an Air Force officer. Your career, your loyalty to it, your love of flying and the sky, are all a part of you. I'm the one who should be sorry, for deluding myself and you into thinking it could be any other way."

Kent felt a quick rush of regret. "Please don't say that. We can get through this together."

"I've been sitting here for hours wondering why I let myself, and let you, think that the world was going to change the rules just for us. And you were wrong about me—I'm not strong at all. At least not strong enough to put myself back to square one and start that shaky path down the runway to land where I may." She shook her head and rose from the couch. "I can't go through it again."

"This isn't the same thing."

"Yes, it is. It's just too similar for me to ignore."

"There's one big difference this time." Kent's face relayed what was in his heart. "You love me, Beth."

"I may," she admitted, flashing him a brief glance that was her undoing. The intensity of his gaze pleaded with her to change her mind. She disciplined her voice. "I loved David and couldn't save him."

Kent bit down on his lip. "I couldn't either." He heard Beth sob and took a deep breath to steady himself. "But what we have together only comes along once, and it's not meant for anyone else but the two of us to share. What happened in the past should prove to us that we need to grab onto the future with both hands and never let go."

He had such a fierce, confident way about him that she almost believed his words. She reached back and summoned the last bit of strength she had. "No, it's not possible."

Kent stepped forward, his face close to her now, so close it filled her vision. She could see the tiny crinkles of lines at the corners of his eyes, the faint worry lines on his forehead, the dark thickness of lashes, and the despair his eyes were helpless to conceal. She reached up and traced a path from the corner of his eye to his temple. "When I saw you in my aunt's room, in your flight suit, I wanted to rip it from your body. But I knew it wouldn't make a difference. I can't go on pretending anymore." She dropped her hand and balled it into a fist at her side. "I guess I was living in a dream, thinking that as long as you didn't put on that Air Force uniform, reality couldn't touch us."

"Nothing will."

"The real world always wins. Planes crash, submarines sink, boats burst into flame. I can't be one of those people who pretend that everything is wonderful, when the eternal knot in my stomach will always tell me otherwise."

"I know what happened at Indian Springs was devastating to you. I wish I could wipe it all away."

"I don't want your pity." She brushed a thumb under one eye. He was not going to see her cry.

"I'm not giving any. Pity is for people who have no hope. You're not one of those people unless you want to be."

"Then what are you trying to give me?"

"I don't know. Maybe I'm trying to give something to me; another chance." He was startled by the sound of his own voice. As his adrenaline level began to rise, he suddenly became angry. "One thing I do know for sure is that I don't intend to continue competing with a ghost. Especially a ghost who didn't even give you the chance to find out the truth."

"What truth?" Tension screamed through her nerves and her chin started to quiver. She had to grit her teeth to control it.

"From what I saw back then and what I've learned now, you may have loved David Mays, but I don't think you were *in* love with him."

"That's ridiculous."

"Is it? Look into your heart." Impulsively, he kissed her. "When he kissed you, did you feel what you felt just now?"

Beth refused to answer. "Did you come here to humiliate me?"

"I came here to make you admit what you already know."

Beth's eyes, now the deep blue color of a sudden ocean storm, the high, proud, tilt of her chin and the stern pout of her lips radiated her anger. "And what is that?"

"That our love developed naturally, right from our hearts. It isn't the same as what you had with David Mays."

The words seemed to upset her control. Her mask slipped for a brief second, and revealed the true face beneath it. Kent started to touch her cheek, but her eyes warned him not to, so he curled his fingers and dropped his fist to his side. "And while I'm asking you to admit things," Kent continued before his courage completely ran out, "I guess I'd better do some confessing of my own. I also came here to bury David."

"That happened a long time ago. There's no need."

"Maybe physically. But emotionally he's still here. I've put this off much too long. We have to talk about it."

" 'It?' "

"Yes, it. The accident, the malfunction, the crash. There's something you need to know, something you need to hear."

Beth took two angry strides away from Kent, turned and exploded as if on impact. "*Malfunction.* What a stupid word that is!" A tremor touched her lips. "The plane broke, Kent." The pain inside her heart broke through her voice until it wavered noticeably. "But even *you* can't bring yourself to say it, can you? It *broke*. And because it broke, my brother died in a desert in Arizona and took my fiancé and two other men along with him. There was hardly enough remains left at the impact site to identify." Tears ran hotly down her cheeks and she wiped them away with the back of her hands.

Kent raised his hands in a 'don't shoot' pose. He knew that he had gone too far, flown too fast and high. "We're more regulated since the diamond crashed: We're more careful. Even the Air Force concedes that the Navy's flight show is flashier and more dangerous than ours."

Beth laughed out loud at the simplicity of his explanation. "And I suppose if you miscalculate a solo crossover break, it will just be a maneuver malfunction."

No more stalling, Kent's mind ordered. *You've gone this far, tell her everything.* "I'm not a solo, Beth," he said slowly, taking her by the shoulders and making her look at him. "I'm number two, left wing. Same position David held in the diamond."

Beth shook her head as if to clear it. What she swallowed hard wasn't bitterness, it was deep agony. "I—I just-assumed . . ." It was minutes before she moved again. When she did, she pushed his hands away and stepped back. "Please. Just leave." She let out a long breath of air in defeat. "Kent, it was only a fantasy all along." *She wasn't going to cry again,* she told herself. But it became harder and harder to hold the tears in check. "We were two people who came together because we wanted something from each other. And while we were together, we tried to believe that all the things we said were real."

"They *are* real." He cupped her cheek with one hand and felt her tremble at his touch.

"Nothing's real. Not me, not you, not anything we feel. It's all just a big illusion to cover up the fact that only the end is absolute."

"I love you, Beth. I know that's real." His fingers trailed down her temple. "I've never said those words to another woman."

She closed her eyes, her heart aching with grief. "You know, you grow up believing that as long as you love someone, it's all you'll ever need to protect them. Then, one day, you find out that everything you've believed all your life was just a fairy tale." When she opened her eyes, the hurt was deeply set inside them.

"This is no fairy tale, Beth. What we have can last."

"For how long? Tell me," she challenged. "If I say I love you, how long would we have together? A day, a week, a year? How long before something happens?"

"Does it matter as long as we use the time we do have loving each other and making each other happy?"

"Yes, it matters. It matters plenty to me."

"You're willing to throw everything away because love doesn't come with a thousand-year guarantee. What about the time you're wasting because you're afraid to let someone back into your life?"

"I thought that you understood that I need something concrete in my life, something that no one can take away."

"I understand how wonderful we are together and how concrete a future we can build if you let yourself have faith in us."

Slowly, Beth stiffened. "Any strength I have left is earmarked for day-to-day survival. I can't spare any on risks like the one you are asking me to take."

In a surprise move, Ken grasped Beth's arm and led her to the window. "Look out there," he demanded. "You think that's a nice, safe, secure little world? Well, it's not. You could get hit by a passing car, struck by lightning in that open field, or even fall down your own stairs and break that lovely neck of yours. Nothing's absolute. Yet, you would deny your-self a chance at real love and family because you want guarantees. Well, the only thing I can guarantee is my love, and it's all yours."

Beth took a long breath, her sorrow a huge, painful knot inside her. "You belong in the sky and I belong on the ground. We cannot live in each other's worlds without killing a big part of ourselves in the process, and I won't risk that."

"Then I am sorry." A look of tired sadness passed over his features. "Not because I told you that I love you, but because you don't want to accept it from me."

A pain squeezed Beth's heart to near bursting, her feelings raw. It was better that Kent thought she didn't care rather than sacrifice the life he loved. "We just weren't meant to be together," she said with a sad smile.

"I can't accept that."

"I'm afraid you'll have to. I have no more to give."

"I have a few days. I'm not giving up. I love you. I want you in my life." He bent forward, and kissed her with hard determination before turning away to walk swiftly to the door.

He grabbed the door and yanked it open. Then, turn-ing back, his mouth moved in a quick, hard smile. "You belong with me and you know it," he said before pulling the door closed behind him.

For a long time, Beth stood there. She had done the right thing by sending him away, she told herself over and over, until it became a dull chant in her mind. She was lying when she said she had no more to give. Her love for Kent was deep inside her, bright, warm and alive.

But it was because she loved him so much that she had to lie.

Chapter Fifteen

"What are you wearing to the reception tonight?" Annie asked after securing Beth's signature on some letters.

Beth began purposely arranging the papers on her desk in neat stacks. "I'm not going."

"Not going? Why?" The corners of Annie's mouth pulled down into a frown.

"I have work to do."

Annie slapped her leg and pushed off the desk. "I don't care if you're waiting for a call from the President himself. What about the possibility of Kirkland waltzing in and using all the work you've done on this project as his stepping stone?"

Beth studied her coffee cup for a long moment. Annie was right. If she couldn't salvage a future with Kent, she could at least have a secure future with the firm. "You're right. Of course I'm going, Annie. I'm not going to hand Kirkland the opportunity to pull this agreement out from under me. It's almost over; I only have to finish it off." For an instant Beth was not sure if she was talking about the deal she had been working so hard on with the Congresswoman, or her relationship with Kent. She decided her words really applied to both.

"You know he's going to be there—Clancey insisted on it."

"I know."

"And you know he's going to be looking for you."

"Maybe."

Annie watched Beth try to pull together her best 'and I don't care' look. "I suppose the fifty phone messages, and enough roses to pack a greenhouse, doesn't mean a thing."

Beth leaned back in her chair. "I need someone with his feet planted firmly on Mother Earth. We both know that and accept it."

"Bull. You're sulking. You want that flyboy and you know it. You're just too stubborn to admit it."

Beth's blue eyes grayed like thunderclouds. "I don't sulk, and I'm not stubborn." The ring of the telephone interrupted more explanation. She forced her voice to be smooth. "I'm taking this call and then I'm going home to get ready."

"No, you're not," Annie said, pressing the button that would send the call to voice mail. "You're going to listen to what I have to say."

"I suppose that if I don't, you'll just park yourself in this office in front of me until I do."

Annie blithely ignoring the heavy silence that encased the room. "You can turn your back and pretend this guy never existed, or you can finally admit to yourself that you're crazy about him and go to it like the Air Force does, all ahead full!"

"It's the Navy."

"Huh?"

"It's the Navy that goes all ahead. The Air Force goes full throttle."

Annie drew back far enough to study Beth's face. "Do I detect a waffling of those resolute walls here?"

Beth flushed but remained silent.

"Okay," Annie went on, "Now that we have it all in the open, what do you intend to do about it?"

The frustration came out as a long whistle under Beth's breath. "Nothing. I have to let him go. It's what's best."

"For who?"

Beth snapped her head around, surprised that Annie would even have to ask. "I'm being sensible. It's best for him, of course."

"By sensible, you mean cowardly, don't you?" Beth leaned back in her chair and stiffened visibly, but Annie ignored the body language. "You quote noble causes, but you're taking the easy way out because you're spineless."

Beth threw her hands up in the air and began to rise from the chair. "This conversation is ridiculous."

"No you don't, girl," Annie said so firmly that Beth dropped right back down into the seat, "I'm not finished. I don't think you want to face the responsibility that comes along with committing to someone."

If Beth was defeated before, now she was crushed. How could Annie always see things so clearly? "How can your heart still hurt so much when your mind knows that you're doing the right thing?"

Annie's sassy attitude became tempered with genuine concern. "This could be your heart's way of telling you that just maybe, this time, you are about to blow it big time."

"I'm afraid to love him and afraid not to love him."

"No one can have it both ways."

"I don't know if I'm capable of loving Kent enough to accept who he is and what he does."

"It's who he is and what he does that made you fall in love with him in the first place. A bonafide knight in shining armor like Kent only comes around once in a woman's life—if she's lucky."

Beth's voice became choked with sincerity. "I thought that I loved David, but the feelings I had for him were nothing compared to the way I feel when I'm with Kent. Could this be real? Or do I just want it so badly that I can't tell the difference?"

"Only you can find the answer to those questions. And I suggest you begin tonight. At the reception."

Beth wore a blue silk halter dress tied with a pale rose sash. As she moved among the guests, the material draped around her body like liquid. She wanted Kent to notice her, although she wasn't sure what she expected to do when he did. As their eyes locked, she had to hold herself in check for fear of turning around and running from what she was feeling inside. Kent was in his full dress blues looking utterly handsome. Beth could only stare at him in awe.

She watched as, with a polite toss of his head, he dismissed a young, blond woman who seemed to be hanging on his every word. His eyes only left Beth's long enough to make sure the plate he had been holding was placed back on a passing tray as he walked toward her.

He looked at her until she blushed. "You look wonderful."

"Captain," she replied in acknowledgement. She saw Kent's smile fade enough for her to know it sounded too stiff, much too formal. "Are you enjoying the party?" she asked, her voice warmer.

"I just got here."

"I see you didn't waste any time."

Kent followed the path of Beth's glance in the direction of the blond, who continued to stare at them with impatient but anticipating eyes. "She's an aide from the Congresswoman's staff," he said.

Beth looked back at Kent, ignoring the knot tightening in her stomach. "It looks like you've got your hands full." She began to move around him when he reached out and stopped her.

"I've been dazzling her with facts and figures. I need all the allies I can muster tonight. I understand there's a high level meeting in the morning. It will probably be more like a firing squad, to shoot down our budget for the next fiscal year."

"Will you be there?" she asked in an odd, but gentle tone.

"Can't. But I've sent ahead a detailed report on the accident. I have to report to McGuire by zero six hundred, so I'm leaving for the base tonight." Kent said the words slowly, feeling his way around the conversation. "There's a practice session scheduled for thirteen thirty hours and I want to be fresh. I also have to check out the F-18 with my crew chief. You know how it is, Beth."

"Of course." Bracing herself against the wave of emotion running through her body, she managed a smile. "I wish you luck."

"Is that why you gave me back the amulet?"

"If it is meant to protect, you'll need it when you fly."

Kent reached out and took her hand. "But then who will protect you from all your demons when I'm gone, Beth?"

She paused, unsure of how to answer. This reception was not the time for another clash of views. "I'd better mingle a little. I'll see you later." Before Kent could stop her, she quickly moved away from him.

"Annie was right," Beth muttered, "I am a coward."

"I'm right about what?" Annie asked from behind her.

"It doesn't matter. It doesn't appear as though I'm about to acquire a backbone anytime soon." *At least not when it comes to taking on the United States Air Force, that is,* she thought.

"In case you're interested, Kirkland's been attached to Clancey like a shadow," Annie said. "I'd stick close to her if I were you. It looks like the snake's coiled and about to strike."

"Thanks, I will."

As Beth turned, she saw Kent whirling around the dance floor with the Congresswoman's aide folded into his arms. A pang of jealousy thumped at her heart as they spun a quick circle to the music and the blond threw her head back in laughter.

"There's Jerry," Annie said, looking over Beth's shoulder and spotting one of the officers Kent had brought along with him.

"Jerry?" Curious, Beth glanced over her shoulder and eyed the young man coming toward them.

"Yeah, one of the Thunderbird's ground crew. And he's mine. I've decided to find out just what it is about a man in uniform." Annie put down her glass and extended her arm to him. "Let's see how well these fly-boys can maneuver on the ground."

Wishing she had half the nerve Annie did, Beth sighed and turned her attention to the rich spread on the table. She picked up a china plate rimmed with gold and aimlessly put food on it.

"Wonderful party, Miss Clarke," Congresswoman Clancey said as she came up on Beth's left.

Beth smiled politely. "I think so too."

"As do I." Alex Kirkland stepped out from behind Rose Clancey and handed her another tall, fluted glass. "Here you go, Rose."

"Thank you, Alex."

Rose? Alex? Beth listened to the exchange, using all the restraint she could muster. Annie was right about Kirkland.

Alex did not try to hide the smug look on his face. "Rose has invited me to sit in on her meeting tomorrow morning." He held up his hand. "Only in case she needs something, of course."

"Oh?" Beth's eyes clawed at him like talons. "I'm sure I can handle anything the Congresswoman might need, Alex."

"You will have everything ready, Miss Clarke?"

"Please, after all the time we've worked together lately, call me Beth."

"And then you must call me Rose."

Beth controlled a smile as the expression on Kirkland's face told her he wasn't as happy. "Rose, then. I wouldn't miss the meeting for the world. If I remember correctly, it's in the Marlboro Room, isn't it?"

Before the Congresswoman could answer, Kirkland cut in. "Don't you think the proceedings might be too painful for you, Beth? Rose is going to rehash the accident at Indian Springs. I wouldn't think that you would want to subject yourself to that." His eyes led Beth's to Kent, who was standing a few feet away. "Especially now."

Beth colored visibly in anger, determined not to let him use her pain to further his own career. "I'll be there, Rose. Maybe I can answer some questions about the accident that you can't."

The Congresswoman's smile of surprise turned to one of approval. "Why, thank you. I would appreciate that."

And that was enough for Kirkland. As the music changed from rock to a more mellow sound, he took the glass from the Congresswoman's hand and touched her elbow. "Now if you will excuse us, Beth. Rose has promised me a dance, and I think this would be a good time to collect it."

Beth forced a self-composed smile. "Somehow, Alex, I had the feeling you were going to say something like that."

Kent had been watching them. When he walked over to where Beth was standing, he could tell by the tension in Beth's eyes that she was upset. "Has Kirkland been giving you a hard time?"

"Just the usual."

"I've missed you," Kent said. "Did you get my messages?"

"I though it best to let things cool down a bit."

"Have they?"

Beth shrugged in answer. Just standing next to him, she knew things would never cool down when it came to Kent McReynolds. The most she could hope for was to be able to bear the heat as best she could.

In the background, the band moved into a slow number. "Dance with me?" Kent held out his hand, leaving the choice up to Beth.

As if someone else suddenly possessed her body, she placed her hand in his without the slightest hesitation. In a second they were moving gracefully across the dance floor.

"There hasn't been a day that I haven't thought about rushing into your office and whisking you away until you listened to reason," he whispered against her hair.

As he turned her in a circle she became lightheaded, but she didn't know if it was from the party or from how she felt about Kent's touch. "What reason am I supposed to listen to?"

"We belong together."

"I don't know about that." She tried to still the wild pounding of her heart, half afraid that Kent could feel it right through his crisp uniform.

"Well, I do. Before you, everything I was had no meaning. I never quite realized it until now."

"This has been a very emotional time for us."

"Is that all?"

Beth felt everything go silent inside her. "I—I . . ." She couldn't tell him. She was still so afraid to share her precious life. ". . . I care about you. And I admire your courage and dedication."

"All those things are important, but they aren't enough. And they shouldn't be enough for people like us. I love you, Beth. Some day you're going to realize that you love me, too. And when you do, somehow I'll know it and I'll be waiting for you."

His words made her head spin, her ears buzz. To try to clear the haze that seemed to settle inside her brain, she began to concentrate on the song to which they were dancing. But it became another mistake. The familiar words rang out over and over in her mind as if fate had chosen the tune expressly for this one occasion.

We'll live forever . . .

If only that could be true, she thought. Only memories really live forever. But memories can't take the place of flesh and blood, and warmth and smiles. Smiles like Kent's that lit his eyes from the inside out.

Knowing together, we did it all for the glory of love . . .

Could she do it all for love? Without Kent, her life would soon settle into the same tedious existence it had been before him. One day would drag into the next, one month to the next. Did she really love him enough? Was the song as prophetic as it sounded? Or was she just looking for that one sign that would show her what to do?

When the music ended, Kent released her, took a step backward and bowed slightly at the waist before kissing her hand in a formal gesture that puzzled her. "It isn't over, Beth. Not by a long shot. No matter how much you may try to persuade yourself otherwise, this is not finished."

He walked away from her and she let him. Annie was right—she was a coward. But no man should be expected to wait for a woman to make up her mind about the future. Especially not a man like Kent.

So, if nothing else had come of this night, she finally understood that she had been right from the beginning. Kent was better off without her in his world.

Still, she knew in her heart of hearts that he was probably the best thing that would ever happen to hers.

Chapter Sixteen

On the way back to her apartment, Beth felt cold and numb. Kent would be gone by morning. She turned off the ignition and sat in her car in the dark. If only she could be sure that love was enough to get her through all those takeoffs and landings he would have to make until he was ready to hang up his wings. If only she could be sure that he would accept the fact that she couldn't be brave every time he climbed into the cockpit of his jet. If only she could be certain he would always have the focus and skill he would need to come back to her safely.

Still clutching the steering wheel, she rested her aching head on top of her hands. Her life seemed to be made up entirely of 'if only.' But the big 'if only' seemed to be whether or not she could swallow her stupid pride and admit that it wasn't Kent's career that frightened her. It was love, itself, with its compromises and its contingencies.

She was still fighting herself on that point when her aunt came up alongside the car. "Are you all right, dear?" Gerry had only tapped lightly on the front windshield, but Beth jumped at the sound. "You've been sitting here for quite a while."

Beth pushed opened the driver's side door. "Should you be out here, Aunt Gerry? You've only been home from the hospital for a few days, and the night air is chilly."

"I'm fine," Gerry reassured her. She placed a hand on Beth's cheek. "But you don't look so good, honey."

"I've really made a mess of it this time, Aunt Gerry."

"I guess you and Kent haven't worked things out."

She shook her head. "It's so overwhelming, Aunt Gerry", Beth said as they walked to the porch swing and sat down.

"Then he told you."

"About him being left wing? Yes."

"No, about what he went through at Indian Springs."

"What about Indian Springs?" Now more confusing thoughts joined the thousands that were already scampering around in Beth's mind.

"Oh my. He didn't tell you."

"Tell me what?"

"He feels that David's death was his fault, dear."

"Steven's plane malfunctioned. It said so right in the report." She stared at her aunt, her heart pounding.

"He wanted to tell you himself."

"I didn't give him the chance. Please, tell me."

Gerry picked up her niece's hand and held it tightly. "You think that by denying that you love Kent, somehow you're going to save him from having to make the choice all pilots have to face one day." Her expression grew serious. "But honey, he already had to make that choice some time ago."

"I don't understand."

Gerry took a deep breath and adjusted her smile. "David was supposed to be in the solo position that day at Indian Springs, but Steven put Kent there because Kent asked him to. Kent didn't feel comfortable with some the maneuvers when he practiced in the diamond. He was having trouble with the timing patterns, and wanted more practice before he settled in at left wing. He asked to be put at solo for a while." Gerry's voice dropped to a whisper. "Kent blames himself for our family having to shoulder a double loss. He said that if it weren't for his lack of nerve, David would still be alive."

Beth rose from the swing and wrapped her arms around herself, a heaviness settling in her chest. All this time she had been worried about her pain, she hadn't even bothered to acknowledge that maybe Kent had pain of his own. "Why didn't he tell me?" she cried, yielding to the compulsive sobs that shook her body.

"Probably for the same reasons you can't tell him how you feel."

Beth spun back to face her aunt. "There's more, isn't there?"

Gerry nodded. "Kent should probably be the one to tell you, but I think you've both wasted enough time. When it comes to pride, sometimes it's best if we take a little off both sides." The look on Beth's face told Gerry that she didn't quite understand. And that was just as well. She had given Kent a little shove toward Beth, and now it was time to nudge Beth.

"Kent gave up flying after the accident. Or, more precisely, he *tried* to give it up."

"And he couldn't. He went back. I know that."

Gerry held onto her niece's hands tightly. "In a way, it's the same with you. You have to go back, too."

Beth ran her hand over her wet cheek. "You're saying that I need to love someone with everything I have, because that's what makes our lives worth living."

"That decision has to come from your own heart, Beth. No one can tell you what to do."

"I've been so busy trying to be a hero that I just let one slip through my fingers. I've been a real fool, haven't I?"

"Yes dear, you certainly have."

In spite of the intensity of what she was feeling, Beth had to smile. "You never have been one to mince words, Aunt Gerry."

"Too old to start now!"

"Kent tried to help me, but I kept turning him away. I should have known he would have never forced me to face the situation. He wanted to help me feel it, for myself, inside where it counts. Not on the surface, with only words."

"And do you think he has?"

Beth smiled. It was there, just around the corners of her heart, all along. Now, suddenly, in a breathless instant, it was released.

"The past few hours I've done nothing but think."

"And?"

"And if I listen very closely to my heart, I think it's been trying to tell me all along that I could never love anyone as much as I love Kent. It's the only thing that's real in this changing world." Admitting her true feelings suddenly released Beth from the bonds of her own guilt. "I want to shout it out—from the sky."

Gerry grinned broadly. "What's stopping you?"

A new sense of strength washed over Beth. "There's something that I have to do first."

* * *

The huge conference room was quickly filling with influential members of Congress and their staffs. As Beth watched them file around the heavy walnut desk, she had never felt surer about what she was planning to do. Everyone seemed too busy to notice her new-found sense of serenity, especially Alex Kirkland, who had been following Rose Clancey around like a puppy since he arrived.

"I didn't think you'd show up," he whispered as he prepared a cup of coffee for the Congresswomen.

"Why wouldn't I?"

"It's pretty obvious to a lot of people that you and that pilot aren't exactly strangers."

Beth found a perverse pleasure in Kirkland's remarks.

"Strangers? Odd choice of words, but you're right. We aren't."

"Considering Clancey's expectations, I thought you would stay as far away from this meeting as you could get."

Tossing her head in a gesture of defiance, she chose her words carefully so as not to tip her hand. "You thought wrong. There's no way I'd miss this. I'm going to do exactly what I have to do here today and let the chips fall where they may."

A look of utter surprise crept across his face. "I didn't think you had it in you."

She didn't comment but merely eyed him blankly, turned away and walked to her seat. But as she watched Alex shadow the Congresswoman again she nearly laughed out loud. He really didn't have to work so hard at trying to snatch the deal away, she was about to put the contract and lease right in his lap. She had finally found something more important to her than work: a future with the man she loved. And since that man spent most of his time flying around the country, she would have no use for the assistant vice presidency.

Rose Clancey rapped her knuckles on the tabletop. "I think we should get started. We have a lot to discuss."

Beth stood. "Madame Congresswoman, I'm afraid that time is of the essence here."

The Congresswoman nodded in approval. "I quite agree."

"With your permission, I would like to get things right out in the open."

"Highly irregular, but because of your personal involvement in this matter, I will allow it."

"Thank you." Beth turned her attention to the faces before her and felt an intensely serious expression settle on her own face. "Distinguished guests, we do not live in a perfect world. Although terrible things do happen, we can never forget that out of tragedy comes new avenues of hope and growth. Captain McReynolds cannot be here today, and although you have his report, there is no way that black lines on white paper can truly tell you what happened that day in Arizona." She looked at each person in turn before saying softly, but firmly, "But I can."

Congresswoman Clancey frowned. "Miss Clarke, I think that it would be best if we returned to the agenda. If you remember, I invited you here to . . ."

"I know very well why I was invited here." Beth heard the sarcasm in her own voice. "And it isn't going to work." Ignoring the Congresswoman's shocked and unfriendly stare, Beth moved to the opposite end of the conference table. "Ladies and gentlemen, I know you have your own concerns about the Blue Eagles, especially with the safety of their program. I want you to know I lost two members of my family in the crash at Indian Springs."

A low rumble rose from those present. A few heads turned and made quiet comments to those sitting beside them.

Rose Clancey quickly called for order. Sensing that her own plan was in danger of failing, she was the next one to speak. "I think that will be enough, Miss Clarke."

A white haired gentleman with soft eyes and the biggest bow tie ever constructed was sitting to Beth's left, and he spoke up in her defense. "Rose, you invited us to this meeting to hear the facts." His hand swept toward Beth. "This young lady can tell us things that can't possibly be contained in this fifty-plus page report you expected us to read. I, for one, would like to hear what she has to say."

A rumble of agreement rose from the floor, and Rose Clancey had no choice but to allow Beth to finish.

Beth nodded to her ally, took a deep breath and began. "My brother, Steven, was 'the boss'. Eagle One. My fiancé was left wing, number two. It took me a long time to be able to talk about that day without flinching, I can't lie to you about that. But they both loved what they did. Each man flying the diamond that day loved what he did. If any of them were here now, there is no doubt in my mind that they'd each do it all over again."

She began to pace with nervous energy, conscious that every eye in the room was following her movements. As the words flowed, her strength grew.

"The question that is probably on everyone's mind is, how could three experienced pilots follow one man to the ground; to their deaths?" Beth could see heads nod in agreement. Now it was up to her to try and answer. "I must have asked myself that question a million times since Indian Springs. It wasn't until recently that I had the courage to face what I knew was the only answer. David, my fiancé, always said to me, 'the Boss is my life and my world, whether I'm upside down or right side up.' What he meant was, it made no difference where the ground was; he had confidence in his ability to fly and in the commander's ability to lead. Every pilot ever trained knows the value of team work and believes in that team's capability to follow orders without question. In the event of war, it's that confidence that just might save a life."

"But it was that team work that caused the deaths at Indian Springs, didn't it Miss Clarke?" Rose Clancey was not about to lose her edge, even if it meant making Bethany Clarke break down in front of everyone in this room. "Your brother made a judgment error and could not react in time to correct it."

The black veil moved painfully at the back of Beth's mind. "No, I believe that is not entirely true."

Rose turned and declared open warfare. "How could you possibly make that statement? You weren't there."

"But I *was* there, Madame Congresswoman. Maybe not in the cockpit, but I was there with them nonetheless, in spirit, in support and in pride. And I saw it all." She drew a deep breath and fought for control.

Everyone in the room seemed to freeze mid-breath. All eyes turned to Beth, and waited to hear what she would say next.

"That day, all eyes, including my own, were on my brother. I was on the ground watching the practice session. And, along with each man in the diamond, we were all waiting for Steven to turn his plane under so the formation would move in unison. With faith in their abilities, in their leader and in their jets, those men died. Running the risk of sounding callous, it's the very loyalty needed in the men of today who are pledged to protect this great country of ours in any situation at any given time."

"But still, it was the stunt flying that caused the deaths." The voice came from the rear of the conference room.

"That is not totally correct." Beth said the words firmly, with the certainty of someone who would never be satisfied until every person in the room understood exactly what happened. "When you read the official report, you'll find that the Air Force feels it was a malfunction in the aircraft itself that caused the lead plane not to be able to respond." There, she said it. She actually said it, and it didn't sound like an excuse anymore. "A tiny piece of metal had come loose and had jammed itself in what is called the 'horizontal stabilizer relief cylinder'." Some confused faces prompted Beth to explain, "It's the part of the plane that brings it level. When it broke off, it wouldn't have mattered if that plane were being flown by one of the Blue Eagles, or another pilot during routine practice, or a fighter pilot in actual combat. It could have happened any time, anywhere, to anyone."

She needed to stop, take a deep breath and swallow the lump that was in her throat. That's exactly what her brother always said to help her stop worrying. Now she was using his words to try and save a little part of him from dying out completely.

Rose Clancey knew her hold on the Blue Eagles' budget was slipping. "Captain McReynolds explained all that to us in his report. I still think it makes no difference."

"Perhaps not to you, Madame Congresswoman, but it does to me and to the quarter of a billion people the Blue Eagles fly over at air shows. Plus, there is something that most of you don't know, something that

Captain McReynolds didn't put in his report. To him it's not a reason to keep the team in the air, but to me it is. And it should be to each and every one of you, too."

"And what might that be?" Clancey asked coldly.

"Captain McReynolds was part of that ill-fated team." Whispers filled the air like the low drone of bees as Beth went on. "He was supposed to be at left wing, but my brother put him at the solo position. That choice is the only reason Captain McReynolds is alive today and my fiancé is not. And even knowing the dangers, Captain McReynolds went back to the sky. And I'm asking you to keep him there, along with everyone else who has ever or will ever put the Blue Eagle emblem over their hearts."

Beth noticed the room was deathly quiet, as still as the moment just before the dawn. As all eyes stayed on her, an image focused in her memory. She could see the Blue Eagles overhead, flying line abreast, trailing red, white and blue smoke from the show canisters, and she knew it was time to paint that picture for the people in the room.

"When I watched the diamond fly to its death, a part of me died with it. It took a long time and the help of many special people to get me to see past my anger and admit that no one could have prevented what happened that day. But now I see much more clearly than I ever have before. No one was to blame. There is simply no one to punish." Beth's voice was full of strength, ringing with a sense of purpose. "When people come out to see the Blue Eagles, they see America—the triumph of our country in the pursuit of happiness." Her next words came right from her heart. "If Norman Rockwell were to have painted a Blue Eagle pilot, he would have painted a small boy, holding a toy plane and looking up at a jet making a vapor trail in the sky. That's where all pilots come from, you know, the dreams of small boys."

She turned and looked the Congresswoman squarely in the eye. What Beth had to say next was really just for her. "And please think about this, Madame Congresswoman. All the tax money shouldn't always go to build nuclear weapons, to arm other nations, or for some politician's pet project. There ought to be some spent on something for the American people."

A wonderful feeling of determination was rising inside her. The floodgates opened and the words just poured out. The hopeful light in her eyes seemed to reach out and touch each person in the room as she continued with her plea.

"The people who support the government and the military deserve something to be proud of, something to believe in and something to dream about, just like that little boy with the toy plane. The Blue Eagles are like a thank you bouquet that can be shared by everyone in this country of ours."

One thought barely crossed her mind before another entered. But Beth carefully selected a few knowing that it was time to deliver the last pitch that just might convert some of these non-believers. "If Steven and David had somehow survived that crash, I know in my heart they would have gotten back in the cockpit and told the world how lucky they were to be flying for the team. And they would have been the first to tell you to keep that team flying. Maybe the Blue Eagles aren't the American Dream, but I can tell you, they are the Dream of America. Don't kill that dream now. Thank you." Beth took a long deep breath and tried to relax. It was up to the people in this room now. She could only hope that she had gotten through to a few.

But her nerves tensed immediately when no one

moved, no one spoke. She looked from face to face and saw only astonishment. *It hasn't worked,* she thought frantically. *I've lost.*

But suddenly, the white-haired man who had first championed her cause rose to his feet. He bowed slightly in Beth's direction and began to applaud. Then, as if on cue, one by one, each person joined him until the room was filled with cheers of support.

Tears of joy found their way into Beth's eyes. When she turned toward the head of the table, even Rose Clancey was on her feet, and Beth knew that the Blue Eagles would survive.

Now, there was only one more thing she had to do.

Chapter Seventeen

N*ever begin an offensive without a clear-cut plan.* At least that's what Steven always said. But Beth was preparing to launch the biggest offensive of her life without a single clue about what to do once she got to McGuire Air Force base. With security tightened because of the visiting Blue Eagles, a long line of cars stretched in front of her. As she inched along with them toward the guard shack, a line of F-18's roared overhead on their way to maneuvers.

Bracing herself, Beth waited for the rush of tension in her shoulders and automatic tightening in her stomach she had come to expect each time she noticed a vapor trail across the sky. But nothing happened, and she suspected the old fears were gone for good.

Her turn at the booth came long before she had even decided what she was going to say to the sentry. He leaned forward and bent just down enough to look into her car, sweeping both the front and back seats with his eyes as he spoke. "Yes, ma'am. What can I do for you today?"

Awkwardly she cleared her throat. "I need to see someone on the base. It's very important." *Well, that was smooth,* Beth thought, while keeping the off-center smile on her face. *I'm sure this guy will just drop whatever it is he doing and rush me right over to where the Blue Eagles are.*

"Your name?" the airman asked, picking up the telephone and beginning to dial before he even finished speaking. "I'll need to check the pass list."

Beth became uneasy. There was no way she was going to be on the pass list. The list was meant only for family and guests. She straightened the teal tunic top she wore over her matching leggings. If she was going to get thrown into the brig, she might as well look presentable. "Bethany Clarke," she said, hoping there was confidence in her voice.

"Clarke, Bethany," the airman repeated into the telephone. "And the name of the person you wish to see?"

"Captain Kent McReynolds." She tried to look as casual as possible. "He flies with the Blue Eagles."

"Ah-ha, I see." He lowered his voice and whispered into the phone, "Forget it, Al. False alarm," and hung up. Turning back to Beth, an irritated look crossed his face. "Do you know how many you make now? About fifty."

"Fifty what?"

The sentry gripped Beth firmly on her arm and walked her back toward her car. "If we let every young lady inside who said they had to talk to one of the Blue Eagles, the team would never get airborne. You'll just have to wait until tomorrow and then get on line after the show."

Ignoring the mocking look on his face, Beth became determined. "But they are here now, aren't they?"

"Of course they are." He cocked a thumb upwards as a chevron of six jets passed overheard. "They're upstairs."

Beth craned her neck just in time to chance a quick glimpse of the passing jets. It was the Blue Eagles all right, the black feather pattern on the belly of the planes was plainly visible as they streaked by.

"But skyborne or parked, fact remains, you can't go in unless you're on the pass list. Pull ahead and turn around. You can't stay here," he said as the phone rang.

Beth pressed both hands over her eyes. She was getting nowhere. The airman was probably reporting her license plate to base security. It was apparent that if she was going to get to see Kent, she would have to sneak onto the base to do it.

Just as she began to drive away, the sentry jumped out and waved his arms to stop her. "Sorry Miss Clarke, I didn't realize who you were." He seemed embarrassed, almost apologetic as he touched the brim of his cap in respect. "Park there. A car will be here to take you to the airfield."

By the time she was escorted to the airfield, the theme from *Star Wars* was blaring out over the loudspeakers. Though this was just a practice, a few hundred people with lifted heads and hand-shaded eyes were out watching the show. Number Eight, the show's narrator, was explaining the Bomb Burst Crossover through the microphone, a maneuver in which four of the F-18's fly directly at one another at an ungodly speed before passing at different levels. Even Beth's escort stopped to watch as they planes passed each other right at show-center.

As the small crowd craned its collective neck, Six went off to the right, doing aileron rolls to distract the spectators, as Five sneaked in from the left, treetop low, creating an ear-splitting roar as he passed overhead. The entrance was designed to surprise the people and, as it did, the narrator quickly announced that all pilots had to learn this tactical maneuver.

"Whew, I'll bet that'll get the Congressmen's attention tomorrow," Beth's escort quipped with a grin.

Beth gave him a returning smile that reached her heart. "You don't know the half of it."

Above them, with *Chariots of Fire* as background music, the jets performed more complicated moves. Barrel Rolls; the Knife-Edge Pass; Catch-ups; Pitch-ups, all narrated in full detail. Even though Beth had seen the moves dozens of times, the effect still dazzled her.

"Yes ma'am," her escort said as all six Blue Eagles above them did a Delta Roll and a Clover Loop, trailing red, white and blue smoke, "looks like a giant waterfall cascading from the sky, doesn't it?"

His words make her look skyward. "It is beautiful," she said as the jets prepared for another move.

Then, as she watched, everything inside her seemed to go silent. Overhead, the two solos broke off as the four planes shot straight up to the top, in perfect formation, just like the last time she had seen it. And now, once again, the man she loved was Number Two, left wing. Finding it impossible to steady her erratic pulse, it suddenly became the worst moment of all— that breathless instant just before all four planes were to turn under and level off. As she watched, a hundred years seemed to pass, but in that one frozen moment, the F-18's rumbled by, having turned safely.

She watched as the planes cut the smoke from the show canisters, appearing as though they had become suddenly unhooked from the sky. Beth felt a wonderful sense of going home again. She unclenched her fingers and flexed them to relax the tension. She felt happy, and almost invincible.

Walking toward the edge of the runway, she could see the six Blue Eagles taxi in and line up in an angle in the show park. Blowing smoke one more time, the pilots opened their canopies, took off their helmets and put on their aviator glasses as a gathering of people lined up for post-show autographs and pictures.

She got in line to meet Number Two, and watched as he accommodated each person's request whole-heartedly. He looked so handsome, with a touch of young boy in his smiling face. Even though he'd only been gone one day, she had nearly forgotten just how beautiful he was in so many ways. Her heart began to pound just from seeing him again.

A small boy of about seven asked Kent to sign his model F-16. Kent dropped to one knee to steady the boy's plastic plane on his thigh before signing his name beneath one wing. With excitement shining all over the young boy's face, the child turned around and smiled up at his father. Beth wouldn't have had to even see that face to know the young boy had already made up his mind to join the Air Force and be a Blue Eagle someday.

As Kent finished the autograph, Beth stepped out from behind one of the spectators. "Why, you're as pretty on the ground as you are in the air, Captain."

Kent froze in his tracks, afraid that his eyes were playing tricks on him. He stared at her, not knowing if, when he spoke, she would vanish like a disappearing vapor trail.

"Quite a following you have. I suppose a girl from the green world doesn't have much of a chance with someone from the sky." She touched the huge Blue Eagle patch on his flightsuit near his heart. "Looks wonderful on you, Kent."

He covered her hand with his. "Do you mean it?" he asked.

She nodded. "I guess I have been a bit stubborn." Her smile didn't stay, but her eyes sparkled. "But we don't have to talk right now." She glanced over her shoulder. "These people came to see you."

Tenderly Kent caressed her face. "Beth . . ."

She placed her forefinger across his lips. "Shh. Don't say anything. Just listen. I love you, Captain McReynolds."

He couldn't contain his smile. He beamed. "Say it again."

"I love you, Kent."

That was all he had to hear. Something inside him said, *Forget military protocol, grab her!* And he couldn't have stopped if he tried. In one motion, he pulled her into his arms as the shouts and hoots from his fellow Blue Eagles and the crowd overpowered even the loud music playing in the background.

Suddenly he held her away and shifted uneasily. "I can't give up flying, Beth."

A secretive smile curled up on her lips. "I don't want you to." She kissed his nose. "You were right. I shouldn't expect any guarantees. I should savor every moment we have together. I love you," Beth said, losing herself in the warm fire in his eyes. "And you loving me is the only guarantee I need."

"Hey, McReynolds," number Four shouted, "I would warn the lady about the penalty for defacing U.S. Government property, but it seems like this time U.S. Government property is defacing a civilian!"

A low roar of laughter rippled across the crowd as Kent pulled Beth behind his jet. "There's more privacy here," he said kissing the corner of Beth's mouth.

"I've been going crazy ever since you left, Kent,"

Beth admitted. "I don't know why I was allowed on base, but somehow they let me in."

"Simple. I put your name on the pass list. I was hoping you'd come. No, it was more like I was *praying* that you would."

Kent's words made her so happy that she actually felt light-headed. "I couldn't let you leave without me."

A brief flash of reality quickly reminded Kent that Beth should be at the office. "Hey, shouldn't you be nailing that deal with the Congresswoman and getting that promotion?"

Beth shook her head. "I'm where I'm supposed to be. Besides, I don't know if I still have a job."

"Why?"

"Let's just say that I've jumped ship. With a little luck, the Blue Eagles are going to be flying for a very long time to come."

"How can you be sure?"

"After I said what had to be said at the meeting, even the Congresswoman was on her feet, applauding."

"You put your career on the line for me?"

"I'd be a fool to trade you for a promotion." Beth ran her hands over his shoulders to his chest. "Besides, someone had to champion the cause while you guys were up in the air doing all that Air Force glitz. It was up to me to defend your honor. This is a new century, you know. All the heroes aren't guys anymore."

"There is one thing." Kent's face went suddenly serious. "The Blue Eagles are leaving for Arizona right after the show."

Beth didn't hesitate. "I want to go with you."

"Are you sure that's what you want?"

"I've never been more sure in my life."

A smile came to life on his lips. "Then marry me."

"I will, but only on one condition."

Kent looked fully into her eyes. "Name it and it's yours."

"I want a diamond." She glimpsed at the sky just over Kent's shoulder. "And it has to be the biggest, bluest diamond anyone has ever seen."

Epilogue

Indian Springs, Arizona—six years later

Overhead the jets made a final pass as the ceremony ended and the crowd began to disperse. Bethany McReynolds adjusted the brim of her large straw hat and waited until nearly everyone had gone before leaving the platform. It had taken her a long time, but through the help of the memorial fund she and Kent had set up, after his tour with the Blue Eagles was over, she had finally gotten her blue diamond.

It glistened in the hot desert sun just to her right. Almost six-feet-tall and made of the finest marble in the country, this diamond was erected on the very spot the ill-fated Blue Eagle team had concluded their tour together in tragedy.

"Mommy, tell her," a sandy-haired little boy of about five said after tugging on her skirt, "tell her that the man on top of that," he pointed to the peak of the diamond, "is Uncle Steven."

"Who wants to know?" Kent walked over and slipped his arm around Beth's shoulders. He picked up his son and gave him an affectionate hug.

"Cindy McGee." The little boy said, pointing to a curly haired girl about the same age. "She doesn't believe me."

Beth watched as Kent extended his hand to the tiny girl and walked with them to the diamond. "Cindy," he said softly, "Kenny's right. That man on the top is his Uncle Steven."

"That's my second name," Kenny shouted, hugging Kent around his neck. "Kent Steven McReynolds."

"Cindy!" a voice from near the cars called out, "We're leaving."

Kent waved a hand in acknowledgement. "I'll take Kenny with me while I drop off Ted's daughter, and then I'll get Joey from your aunt and uncle. You stay here for a while, Beth," Kent said glancing up at the carved faces on the front of the stone. "Maybe you would like to be alone for a few minutes. As soon as I get the kids settled, I'll be back."

Beth nodded. She did have a few things she wanted to say to her brother and to David. She looked up at the diamond. At each point was a likeness of the pilots in their positions, with their names carved beneath. In the center of the monument was the diamond formation of F-16's, pointing upwards toward heaven, where she knew they all were.

A great exhilaration filled her. "Steven," she whispered, "maybe somehow you knew that something was going to happen that day. I'll always remember it was *you* who saved Kent's life."

She felt Kent slip his arms around her waist and she leaned back into his chest. "You won't be able to put your arms around me much longer," Beth said, spinning in his arms to face him. "Soon I'll be showing."

He moved a hand to face her and cupped her chin. "I like when you're pregnant. It makes a statement."

Beth linked her arms around his neck. "Just how many statements do you intend to make?"

His brows flicked a little in playful amusement. "Six, maybe seven."

"Why not eight? That's enough to make up an entire Blue Eagle team!" She smiled at him with a hint of challenge in her eyes.

"Not a bad idea."

Beth stepped back and looked down at her slightly rounded stomach. "Maybe this one will be a girl." She looked back up at him with dreamy eyes. "Do you think she'll be the first female Blue Eagle pilot?"

"If she's as tenacious as her mom, I think so."

Kent drew her hands away from his neck to hold them in his own. "Right after the accident I stood on this very spot. It was dawn, and I had never felt so alone in my life. I was sure that I could never feel whole again. I never imagined that my life was saved for a reason." He pushed a stray lock of hair from her eyes. "But it was."

She raised his hand to her cheek. "I am so lucky to have you, to have the kids. Coming back here only makes me realize how lucky we both are." She gazed back up at her blue diamond. "When it happened, I thought I'd lost everything." She brushed her hand over the face of the monument. "Instead, because of it, I found everything."

Beth looked up into the clear, blue desert sky, the kind of sky made just for flying. And over Kent's shoulder, above the diamond, she could swear that for a brief moment, Steven and David were standing in the clouds giving her a thumb's-up in approval.